SECURING IT ALL

THE PUNISHMENT PIT ~ BOOK TWO

LIVIA GRANT

Published by Black Collar Press

Securing it All
Punishment Pit Series - Book Two
by Livia Grant

e-book ISBN: **978-1-947559-34-9**
Print ISBN: **978-1-947559-35-6**

Cover Art by Laura Hidalgo and Spellbinding Creations

Sign Up for Livia's Newsletter! www.liviagrant.com/newsletter/

First Electronic Publish Date, September 2020

First Print Publish Date, September 2020

DEDICATION

To my fellow kinksters out there. Whether you're in a 24/7 M/s relationship or just love getting your dose of kink in the pages of racy novels—or honestly, anywhere on the BDSM continuum in between— you are my people.

Punishing his wife for her mistakes was the right choice.
Having his best friend handle it definitely wasn't it.

Choosing dominance should be easy.
But Markus has been torn apart by betrayal,
twisted up and confused by all the dark lies.

His and hers. A matching set.

But leaving Brianna at The Punishment Pit didn't help.

Lukus has always been the Master's Master.
Permanent bachelor and hardcore dom,
yet seeing Brianna's submission has him wanting more.
But she's forbidden fruit, his best friend's wife,
and a good man would help them fix this mess.

Everything is a gamble. A game of pain and pleasure.
Would they get their second chance?

CHAPTER ONE

LUKUS

Lukus's BMW hugged the exit ramp from the expressway at close to double the posted speed. He'd decided to take his pent-up sexual frustration out on his car and was grateful the Saturday afternoon traffic was light. In his condition, if the traffic were any heavier, someone could end up hurt.

He'd never been to Markus's house out in the suburbs, and the anger he'd suppressed for three years was beginning to resurface with each passing mile. It was bad enough that Markus had never invited him over. No. His best friend actually had the balls to request someone else come out from Lukus's company to install the security system during construction of the multi-million-dollar home. By the time it was finished, Markus had married Brianna. Lukus hadn't even been invited to the wedding.

My invitation must have been lost in the mail.

Thinking back to his friend's marriage didn't improve Lukus's mood. Markus had all but dropped Lukus once Brianna had entered his life. Lukus had gone to see Markus at his office one evening after the couple had gotten back from their honeymoon, hoping for an explanation. He'd been moderately drunk. Words had been exchanged and punches thrown. After that, the men had gone nearly a year without speaking.

Only Lukus's arrest two years ago had brought them back together again. Markus had really come through for him when the chips were down, and while his friend had insisted on keeping Lukus hidden from his wife, he'd just been relieved to resume their friendship. The men had lunch together at least once a week and texted even more frequently. The friends had come to an unspoken truce, agreeing to avoid the subject of Brianna, and why Markus walked away from the BDSM lifestyle.

And now, the last twenty-four hours had pretty much torn down all of the walls holding Markus's secrets at bay. While Brianna had answered some of the questions that had been gnawing at Lukus for years, the knowledge didn't alleviate Lukus's anger. He understood that Markus only sought to protect Brianna from the memory of the abuse she'd experienced, but did he somehow think that

Lukus was anything like the bastard who'd abused his wife?

What the fuck did he think I was going to do? Show up at the wedding in leather, whip in hand, and scare the shit out of her?

Lukus wasn't sure what he was going to find when he got to his friend's house. He also didn't have a clue how he was going to look Markus in the eye given his magnetic attraction to Brianna. Just thinking of her tied naked in his bed with her pink, striped ass and bound breasts still had his cock throbbing with desire.

Maybe Markus was right to keep her away from me after all. If I was back at my loft, I'd probably be fucking her silly by now.

Thankfully, he'd had enough willpower to get the hell out of there before he did something stupid. Just thinking of her again reminded him to make a call he'd meant to make as soon as he got on the road.

He dialed Derek. His friend answered quickly.

"Hey," his partner asked. "How's the training going? Did she sign the divorce papers yet?"

Lukus should have been prepared for the question. "No... not yet and honestly, I don't think she's going to. I'm on my way out to talk to Markus about it now. That's why I'm calling. What's Rachel up to this morning?"

Derek laughed. "Well, right this minute she's

kneeling under the desk at the office sucking me off. Why?"

"We've discussed this, man. You need to stop bringing her into the security office to service you. All it does is get the rest of the crew all horny and jumpy. Unless you plan to start sharing her, you need to cut that shit out."

"Hey, it's Saturday and I already sent the guys working today out on their assignments. No one is around right now and even if they come back, she can just stay hidden at my feet under the desk."

"Fine, but as soon as you're done defiling your wife's throat, I need you to send Rachel up to my loft to babysit."

Derek chuckled. "What? Did you have some chick show up with a kid she's trying to saddle you with?"

"Don't be an ass. I left Brianna tied up to my bed. She gets upset when she's left locked up. She's terrified of being stuck in case the building catches on fire or some bullshit like that. Honestly, at first, I laughed it off, but when I really think about it, I realize we might be putting the submissives in danger when we tie them up and leave them unattended. You think you could send Rachel up to sit with her until I get back?" There was silence on the phone for a few long seconds. "Derek.... you still there?"

"Let me get this straight. You, Master Lukus Mitchell, the hard-ass owner of The Punishment

Pit, not only took a sub that you were charged with punishing up to your private loft, but you have her tied to your soft, king-size bed. And now you want my sub... my *wife*... to go keep her company so she doesn't get scared. Is that really what you're saying here?"

"I told you... You know what? Fuck it. I'm sorry I called." Lukus was suddenly self-conscious. Calling Derek seemed like a fine idea before, but now hearing his words coming back at him from his second in command, he sounded exactly like one of the lightweight Doms that he and Derek liked to make fun of—the ones that brought their subs into the club because they were too soft to actually discipline them properly themselves.

Lukus could hear muffled sounds at the other end of the connection. He then heard Derek telling Rachel to go kneel out in the reception area and wait for him. After a few seconds, Derek was back on the line and Lukus could hear the concern in his voice.

"Alright man. What the hell is going on with you? Please tell me you didn't fuck her."

Lukus wanted to be pissed at his friend for even thinking it, but he knew he'd be a complete hypocrite if he busted Derek's balls over his accusation since it had taken all his restraint not to claim Brianna. He took a deep breath and sighed before answering truthfully. "No, man. I didn't fuck her. But I'll tell you... I wanted to... *bad*. I had

5

to get the hell out of there before I did something stupid."

"Shit. Well, yes. Fucking Markus's wife would have been colossally stupid. She's hot, but she's so off limits."

"Tell me something I don't already know. Listen, will you please send Rachel up? I don't want her to even know Rachel is there and under no circumstances do I want Rachel talking to her. Do you hear me? Bri knows next to nothing about Markus in his Dom days and I don't need Rachel filling her in yet. Got that?"

"Sure, I can send her up and she'll do what I tell her. You know that. I'm worried about you though. This isn't like you at all. I hear it in your voice, Lukus. You're getting emotionally invested in this."

"Well, fuck yeah. How the hell can I not after the history Markus and I have had since he met Brianna? There's a part of me that's relieved he's turning to me to help him... like the old days. Then there's a part of me that's furious that I wasn't good enough to be part of their lives before this. He waits until some asshole fucks her and now, she's suddenly my problem? But the biggest part of me is pissed because he's trying to throw away something that he should have been taking better care of. Maybe if he'd communicated more with his wife, she never would have felt the need to cheat on him or gotten wrapped up in this sociopath's shit."

"Fuck a duck. You're actually taking her side in this? She must be part witch to have cast a spell on you and get you this twisted up so fast, man."

"I never said I'm taking her side, dammit. I just spent a few minutes doing something Markus should have done a long time ago. It took me all of ten minutes to figure out what the hell is going on. He was either blind or just didn't give a shit to have missed all of the signs of what she needed to be happy."

"And just what is that, Dr. Mitchell?"

"Screw you, man. I'm sorry I called."

"Okay... I'm sorry. I'll back off. I'll send Rachel up and we can talk about all of this shit later when you get back here. Good luck, Lukus. I don't envy you."

"Thanks. I'll call you later when I'm on my way back into the city."

"Later."

Lukus glanced at his GPS to see how much farther he had to go. He was getting close now and decided to call and let Markus know to let him in.

When the phone rang six times and rolled to voicemail, Lukus lost his temper. "Markus, you'd better be up, sober, and ready to listen. I'm almost there. We have a lot to talk about." He cut the call off.

Within five minutes, Lukus was parking in the brick driveway of his friend's mansion. The early spring flowers were just emerging in the landscaped beds lining the wide walkway to the massive front door. Lukus rang the doorbell several times but got no response from inside. He of course tested the door, but it was locked as expected. After knocking on several doors and windows and phoning Markus's cell phone two more times, Lukus was starting to get worried.

Surely, he didn't do something stupid.

Before meeting Brianna, Lukus would have been furious at just the thought of his friend harming himself over a woman. But now, having met Brianna, having held her… hell, he could almost understand the temptation… *almost*.

The next call he made was back to Derek. "Hey man. I need your help. I'm at Markus's house and he's not answering. The house is buttoned up tight, but I need to get in. Can you turn off the alarm from the remote access system and send a command to unlock the front door?"

"Sure… hold on. You don't think he did something, do you?"

Lukus wasn't about to tell Derek the thought had already crossed his mind. "Naw. I'm sure he just drank like a fiend and passed out. I'll probably need to throw his ass into a cold shower to get him sobered up enough to even talk to him."

After a few minutes, Derek was back on the line. "Okay, you should be able to get in now without an issue."

"I'm going in." Lukus tentatively opened the

front door, holding his breath in case the alarm sounded. He was relieved when it didn't. "Thanks, man. I'll call you later."

Lukus quietly closed the door, taking a few seconds to glance around the Italian marble tile of the foyer with the grand circular staircase leading up to the second floor. The floor plan was open, and he could see all the way through to the back of the house. The whole great room sported two stories of huge windows that looked out onto a fairway of the connecting country club's manicured golf course. It was the kind of elegant home he'd expected, yet he pushed down his anger that he'd never been welcome there before.

Loud rock music blared throughout the house and Lukus called out, trying to project his voice over the noise. "Markus, where the hell are you?"

As he moved into the great room, he had to step over several broken vases, picture frames, and even a chair that was now in multiple pieces. The mirror over the stone fireplace was shattered.

Lukus finally found Markus sprawled face down on the couch, his left arm hanging over the side. An empty rock glass was discarded nearby. Lukus walked over and gave his friend a poke. "Hey, man. I've been calling you. Wake up. We need to talk."

Nothing.

Time stood still as Lukus waited, holding his breath. Was he breathing? It scared the shit out of him that for the briefest of seconds he actually thought of comforting Brianna through losing her husband. Luckily, self-disgust shoved the vision aside, knowing he'd be lost without Markus, the man he thought of like a brother, in his life.

Don't be a pussy, Mitchell. Reach out and check his pulse.

Lukus held his breath, afraid he might be too late and even more afraid to examine how that made him feel. When Markus didn't budge, Lukus squatted down in front of him, tentatively reaching out to do a pulse check. A wave of relief washed over him at finding a strong heartbeat. He roughly rolled Markus onto his side, tapping his face to rouse him. The only evidence Markus even knew Lukus was there was a low groan at being disturbed.

His friend looked like shit. His beard had always grown fast and he now had a full day's scruff on his strong jaw. Markus's dark hair looked like it had been through a windstorm and he still had on the same clothes he'd been wearing in court the day before. The only addition to his wardrobe appeared to be dark food or drink dribbled down the front of his wrinkled dress shirt. The normally put-together lawyer was looking anything but lawyerly today.

While Lukus took a minute to glance around the room, he felt Markus push on his leg, moving him out of the way so he could lean over the edge of the couch to puke on the carpet. Lukus managed to jump back just in time.

"Nice. It feels like we're back in college after one of our all-night frat parties. I would've really been pissed if you'd barfed on my favorite boots."

It took a few minutes for Markus to finish and recover enough to speak. He leaned back against the couch cushions, his eyes looking like they were having trouble focusing on Lukus. His voice croaked when he spoke. "What the hell are you doing here? Did you bring the divorce papers?"

Lukus stood stoic, observing his friend for a moment before answering the million-dollar question hanging between them. Only the heavy beat of Ozzy Osborne disguised Lukus's own thumping pulse as he had to admit, "No. I failed you. She isn't gonna sign the divorce papers, Markus."

The wave of tormented relief that washed over Markus's face was telling. "Oh, thank God. I should be pissed... but I'm not. I've dreaded you getting here with signed papers. I know it's what I asked you to do for me, but it guts me just thinking about losing her. I know you're gonna give me all kinds of shit for being a pussy for feeling like this after what she did, but I can't help it. I love her so much it hurts, man."

Lukus looked away. He should have been relieved and happy that his best friend was smart enough to fight for his marriage, but until that very minute, Lukus hadn't been willing to admit that a sliver of himself had hoped Markus would still want out and leave Brianna available, for him.

Don't be an asshole, Mitchell. They love each other. Back the fuck out of this.

Lukus countered defensively, "Hey, I'm not going to say jack shit. In fact, if you hadn't woke up to realize what the hell you're losing by now, I was coming out here to bang some sense into you."

Markus managed to sit up, but he snapped his eyes closed, still looking queasy as Lukus continued. "I really like what you've done with the place. You know, you're gonna have seven years bad luck from the broken mirror."

Markus finally reopened his eyes. He was more focused and turned his sights on his best friend. "Cut the damn small talk. What happened last night and how is she doing?"

Lukus didn't reply right away. Instead he walked over to the stereo and shut it off before heading to a chair opposite the couch and sitting down. The sudden silence felt like a wedge between the men. Lukus tried to delay. "Why don't you go take a shower and we'll talk after. I'll make you some food."

"Stop stalling. What the hell happened to my wife?" Markus's tone had an accusatory edge.

Lukus couldn't help but get defensive. "Hey, nothing happened to your wife you didn't ask to happen and don't forget that. You left her there—

alone—with two men who were going to whip, paddle, and humiliate the shit out of her. How could you do that to her knowing what the hell she's been through in the past? The least you could have done was warn me."

At Lukus's angry words, Markus's previously green hue grew pale.

"I told you everything you needed to know. You didn't need to hear about all the Jake shit. If she was so traumatized by what that asshole did to her, she should have called the police when he showed up at the salon, not jump in a car to meet him and fuck the afternoon away." The torture in his voice was evident.

Both men were silent for a moment while Lukus chose his next words wisely.

"You really screwed this up, Markus. I love you like a brother, but from the minute you met that woman you've done one wrong thing after another to fuck things up and I'm done letting you get away with it."

"What? You're saying it's *my* fault she cheated? Jesus Christ, Lukus! How the hell did she get you wrapped around her little finger so fast? Wait... I forgot. That's what she does. She cries that soft, vulnerable cry and blinks those big brown eyes, or laughs that cute little giggle of hers and it melts your damn heart. I should know. I've seen her do it to every man I've ever introduced her to."

"Is that why you never let me meet her before?

Why you didn't even invite me to your wedding? We were like brothers, Markus. Do you know how ridiculous it is that I just met her for the first time last night?"

Markus stumbled to his feet to walk towards the wet bar across the room. He threw his next insult over his shoulder. "Oh, for Christ's sake. Are we gonna have this argument again? I had my reasons for not introducing you. I thought you understood that."

"I never understood… at least not until today. Would it have killed you to explain it to me back then? It took all of ten minutes of talking with Bri to figure it all out. I would've understood."

"Yeah, right. You were already so angry with me for the way things had ended with Georgie that I knew you'd give me grief over what I had to do to get Brianna to trust me."

Lukus was relieved when Markus grabbed a bottle of water from the small refrigerator in the bar area instead of more alcohol.

"I resent that," he said. "What have I ever done to make you think I wouldn't have supported you marrying Brianna?"

"Are you kidding me? After all the shit you gave me after Georgie left me? You can't help yourself."

"That's completely different. You crossed the line with Georgie. I did to you what I would have done to any Dom in the club who had done what you did. You blew through her safeword—not once, but *twice*. You hurt her, Markus. Were you really surprised she left you?"

Markus took a seat at the far end of the couch away from the foul-smelling mess on the floor. He appeared defeated as he sat quietly, unable to look his friend in the eye. When he finally did, Lukus worried Markus might cry. "I regret losing control that night more than you'll ever know, but Georgie didn't leave me because I blew through her safeword. She was ready to leave me long before that. That was just the final straw. I've been thinking about it all night." He took a swig of water. "I finally had to take a fucking Ambien just so I could finally shut my brain off."

Markus shook his head before continuing. "It's so damn funny, you know? I lost my first wife—a professed submissive when I married her—because I was too dominant for her. I demanded her submission in all things because when we met, that's what she said she wanted. But when it came down to it, she was a part-timer who couldn't live the life. Then I fall in love and marry her polar opposite—a woman who's afraid of dominance, a woman who needed to be protected and pampered. Brianna wanted all the things Georgie never did. I've been like a damn puppy dog with her. Anything she's wanted I've given her. And you know what? I loved every single minute of it. There's nothing I wouldn't do for Brianna. But

15

after all that, she ends up hurting me worse than Georgie ever did."

Lukus was furious, shouting in the new silence. "You're such an ass, you know that? All these years, you haven't been paying attention to me at all, have you? I've been trying to guide you, but you just had to do it your way. I thought after Georgie left, you'd finally wised up, but you didn't get shit. You're still clueless about what it takes to be a Dom."

Markus's face was beet red as his defensiveness kicked in. "Oh, do tell me, Master Lukus. I don't recall you being with the same sub for longer than three months at a stretch... *ever*. So, what the hell makes you some relationship expert?"

Lukus was up on his feet, closing the distance between them in just a few seconds. He grabbed Markus's shirt and pulled him close. "You listen here. I don't know jack about being married, but I know everything there is to know about what makes a good Dom. And buddy, I hate to tell you, but you suck at it. You're truly no better than Jake is and honestly, right this minute, I think Brianna deserves better."

Markus's face clouded with anger. "Fuck you, Lukus. In case you haven't noticed, I'm not her Dom. I'm her *husband*. There's a difference."

"For some people, maybe, but not for men like us, Markus. Brianna *needs* a Dom. She *wants* a Dom and you totally let her down."

Markus shoved Lukus until he had to release

his hold on his still seated friend. "That's bullshit. You should have seen her shake just thinking about what that asshole did to her. Even months later she was still a nervous wreck. We didn't even have sex for the first two months we dated—which is a lifetime for me. I waited for her to be ready because she was special."

"Well, finally. Something we can agree upon. She is special. She's very special." Lukus's voice was shaking with emotion that even a stranger would pick up on.

Markus's eyes narrowed at his friend's words. He stumbled to his feet and shouted in his friend's face. "What the hell? Did you fuck my wife?"

CHAPTER TWO

MARKUS

M arkus didn't think he could take any more betrayal. Brianna cheating had almost killed him. The thought of his best friend betraying him too... his heart clinched, the pressure making it feel like it might explode.

The old friends were only inches apart from each other when Lukus shouted in his face. "Screw you, Markus. I did *not* fuck your wife... but you know what? I wanted to. I might have even done it too if she would have let me, but she loves you so much she wouldn't hear of it."

Conflicting emotions made it impossible to think. Grateful Brianna and Lukus hadn't done the unthinkable, his friend's confession hurt. The only thing that tempered the pain was the thought that Brianna still loved him.

Still furious, Markus shoved Lukus backwards with both hands. "You sonofabitch! I can't believe I was stupid enough to leave her there with you. I should have known you wouldn't be able to keep your dick in your pants."

Lukus rushed back up on Markus and retook him by the collar of his stained shirt. "I'm going to let that one go because I know how upset you are right now, and I'll be damned if we're going to let anything come between us again. I meant it when I said you're like a brother to me, Markus. So... as your brother, I'm obligated to help you, even when you're acting like a complete asshole."

Lukus roughly pushed Markus back against the couch cushion where he collapsed, defeated. His friend stepped away, warning, "Now you sit there and listen. Keep your fucking mouth shut until I'm done." Lukus started pacing and Markus used the time to try to push down the throbbing in his head, courtesy of the mother of all headaches he'd ever had. He was in need of a toothbrush but could tell Lukus wasn't done lecturing him yet.

Lukus finally stopped pacing, turning towards him and asked, "Did Brianna ever tell you how she met Jake?"

"What the hell does that have to do with anything?" Markus spat.

"Answer the damn question. Did she?"

"Yeah. She said it was at some BDSM club downtown."

"So, you knew then that she had at least some interest in learning more about the D/s lifestyle?"

Markus paused, worried where this line of questioning was going. "Well sure, but that was before that asshole abused her and made her hate it. He made her afraid of the lifestyle."

"I know she told you about what he did back then, but did you ever talk about what she'd seen in Jake in the first place? What she was looking for at the clubs?"

This line of questioning didn't make any sense to him. He snapped defensively, "No. I didn't want to bring anything up that would upset her. She made it clear in the beginning she was afraid of rough play and I knew if I wanted to be with her, I'd need to give up being a Dom. At first I thought it would be hard, but honestly, she made it easy. She's so responsive and loving. Georgie always told me I couldn't be a romantic to save my life. I bet she would shit bricks if she could see how romantic I am... *was*...with Bri."

"So, Georgie complained that you weren't romantic?"

"All the time. But, fuck—I was still going for partner in the firm back then. I was working eighty hours a week. She should have been happy with the great sex, the money, the house, and the trips with her sisters. But it was never enough with her."

"So, you at least admit that just because a woman wants to be a sub, it doesn't mean all she wants is to be paddled, tied up, and fucked while being a slave to cook and clean your house?" Lukus's tone was only half joking.

"Stop being such an ass. You know that's not how I define a good sub, Lukus."

"Do I? That's exactly what I saw you do with Georgie. You didn't really give anything of yourself to her. You provided for her, sure, and you dominated her sexually in the bedroom. But did you ever think that maybe—just maybe—she needed some of the same things you've been giving to Brianna the last three years? You're right about Georgie wanting to leave you before. I could see it. All she wanted was more of your time, Markus. She needed you to *see* her. To *love* her. To *cherish* her. All you did well was dominate her and try to buy her."

This whole conversation was going nowhere. "As riveting as this walk down memory lane is, what the fuck does this have to do with Brianna?"

"It has everything to do with Brianna because you went from one extreme with Georgie to the opposite extreme with Brianna."

"Bri should have been happy with all she had, too! I didn't just give her money, the house, and the salon. No. I didn't repeat the mistakes I made with Georgie. I gave her so much of myself. Why wasn't that enough for her? Why wasn't *I* enough for her?"

Markus's voice cracked as he swallowed hard to keep from crying as he once again faced the fact that his wife had cheated on him.

"I almost understand why Georgie left," Markus continued brokenly. "Almost. But Bri, I gave her my heart and she fucking stabbed it." He felt weak as several tears spilled from his eyes to run down his cheeks.

He hated the pity he saw in Lukus's eyes as he added, "Listen, Markus. I admire you. I honestly do. I never understood how you could just walk away from the lifestyle like you did, but I know now it's because you truly love Bri."

"A lot of fucking good it did me." He wiped the tears from his cheek, disgust on his face for his own weakness. "You have the right idea, Lukus. You don't get tied down with one woman who can gut you. I should have followed in your footsteps. I could be fucking a different woman every night at the club like you."

Lukus let out a long sigh. "Believe me, after thirty-four years, this being single shit is not nearly as much fun as it used to be. Don't envy me. I'd give anything to have what you and James have."

"You mean what I *had*." Even though he said the words, he couldn't believe she was gone.

"It's not too late, Markus. Do you still love her?"

A wave of pain crashed through to touch every part of his body. "I've never loved anything or anyone so much. I feel like half of me died yesterday."

"She didn't die," Lukus answered. "She's alive

and more importantly, she refuses to give up on you and your marriage. I pulled out some pretty heavy-duty punishments that should've made her a simpering mess within an hour and she blew through them all. You have no idea what you have, do you?"

"Other than an adulterous wife?"

"Markus, she went with that asshole because unlike you, she couldn't keep pushing down her natural instincts, and the jerk knew how to prey on those deep-seated needs."

"Have you lost your mind? What needs? To be beaten within an inch of her life?"

"While Jake is obviously an abusive prick, it doesn't change the fact that Brianna has deep submissive tendencies. It's why she went to the BDSM clubs years ago in the first place. And while Jake deserves to be in jail, he did help Brianna in one way. He helped her discover she's a pain slut."

Markus snorted loudly as he let loose with a scoff. "Oh, for Christ's sake. You're losing it, Lukus. Brianna hated how he abused her, how he hurt her. She *hates* pain."

"She hates uncontrolled pain. She hates being subjected to pain from someone who doesn't love or protect her and who she can't trust, but I watched her come twice since last night from nothing more than a strong belting on her ass and pussy. She hit sub-space faster than any sub I've ever trained. It was amazing."

"Shut the fuck up." Markus glared at Lukus as if he were flat out lying.

"Why would I lie, Markus? Think about last night when you were riding her up in the balcony. I arrived in time to realize she was coming completely unglued when you were controlling her, fucking her like the Dom you really are. Don't get me wrong. Brianna isn't even close to a full-timer for the lifestyle, but that doesn't mean she isn't submissive. I've seen how strong she can be, and I actually admire it, but I'm here to tell you there's a part of herself she's been trying to suppress —a part that only Jake's dominance filled for her. She didn't know how to tell you and because you kept the fact you were a Dom secret from her, she never had a clue you might actually understand. She's starving for your strength, Markus.

"And that doesn't mean she wants you to flip over to the way you were with Georgie. In case you haven't figured it out yet, you have both extremes down pat. What you need to do now is blend the two parts of you into one strong Dom who protects his submissive, dominates his submissive, cherishes his submissive, disciplines and loves his submissive."

Markus shook his head in disbelief. "I can't believe it."

"Bri mentioned she likes to read romance novels. Does she read much around you?" Lukus asked.

"Oh, hell yes. She constantly has her nose in her iPad, reading some romance novel or another. She tries to put it down when I'm home to spend more time with me, but on the weekends, I catch her reading all the time. Why?"

"Did you ever take the time to notice what she was reading?"

"Why the hell would I care? What guy wants to read romance novels?"

"Where's her iPad? I'll show you why you should have cared."

Markus got up and stumbled to the kitchen, grabbing Brianna's iPad along with a bottle of water for Lukus. "Here, but I have no idea what this is supposed to prove."

"What it's going to prove is what's at the heart of your problem with both Bri and even Georgie," Lukus said, bringing up the book application on Brianna's device. "Being a Dom means you need to constantly be looking for ways to understand your sub. By their nature, most subs are not able to ask for what they want. They need us to pick up on the subtle cues, about what they want and need. It's how they build trust in their Doms. If they knew how to demand what they needed, they'd be a Domme for Christ's sake. Brianna basically told me that in so many words today."

Markus turned his friend's words over as he waited for Lukus to scroll through the books stored on Brianna's iPad. Could he have been completely blind, missing Brianna's hints about her deepest needs? He didn't think he could feel worse than he had before, but he hated the thought of letting her down.

"Okay, there are a lot of popular erotic novels with strong, dominant heroes on her, but there are also some really hard-core books. Here... Anne Rice's *The Claiming of Sleeping Beauty*." Lukus turned the device around so Markus could see the cover. "That's about as graphic a D/s story as you can read." Lukus then changed apps. "Let's look at her browser history."

He tapped the screen. "See, Markus. The iPad is full of visits to sites dedicated to domestic discipline."

Lukus handed the iPad over to Markus. His hands trembled as he spent a few minutes looking through the books his wife had been reading. He opened *The Claiming of Beauty* to the page-mark that Bri had left the book on and took a few minutes to read.

He could feel Lukus watching him as he read. With each paragraph he read, the faster his heart beat. It felt like a dream... All this time, she'd been sitting next to him... lying in bed at night right next to him... reading... His own cock twitched reading about all of the debauched torments Beauty was going through between the pages—torments that didn't sound terribly different from the horrors she'd been put through at the hands of her asshole ex, Jake.

How could she read this? Markus's mind raced, trying to understand, latching onto the words his best friend had thrown at him minutes before. Was it possible they could somehow salvage their marriage?

"Is it too late? Did I screw this up beyond repair?" Markus finally asked outright.

Lukus grinned at his friend. "Not by a long shot. She's been waiting for you to claim her just like the prince claimed Beauty." Then Lukus got serious, all traces of his smile gone. "And honestly, Markus. If you don't make this right with her, I worry about her. With her tolerance for pain, if she goes out to troll for a new Dom at the clubs, she could really get hooked up with another Jake who could end up killing her. She won't safeword out with her high tolerance for pain. She needs special care."

The thought of someone else touching her ever again enraged him. "Over my dead body," Markus growled. "She's *mine*. No one else is ever gonna fucking touch her again." Markus stared into his friend's eyes before issuing his warning. "And that includes you, Lukus. I can hear it in your voice. You wanna fuck my wife." The thought terrified him.

But Lukus laughed his warning off. "Hell yes, I wanna screw your wife. Have you seen her lately?

She's smoking hot. You have no idea how great you and James have it. You lucky bastards get the wife, the submissive. Hell, you'll even have her popping out babies before you know it. She's smart and the perfect balance of submission and strength. You're rich and successful. You're one of the privileged few who gets to have it all in life. Don't screw this up ever again because the next time you do, I won't be coming out here to help you figure it out. I'll be stealing her away on a plane. I'll take her far away from here and believe me—I'll know how to give her what she needs. Don't do something you'll regret."

Markus should have been pissed, but seeing the levity on Lukus's face helped lift the blanket of dread he'd been wearing since listening to his wife cheating on him the day before.

"That sounds like a threat."

Lukus grinned back. "Hell, no. It's a promise."

The men stood still, awkwardly silent until Lukus walked closer and offered his hand for a shake. A wave of gratitude had Markus reaching out and pulling his best friend into an embrace instead. "Thanks so much for coming out here and knocking some sense into me. Seriously, I really can't thank you enough."

Lukus slapped his back as he answered, "Any time, bro. You dug my ass out of the fire this week, too. It's only fair I repay the favor."

Markus sighed as they stepped back from one another, a new worry forming. "So now what? Do I just come down and collect her and say *'Oops, sweetheart. I made a mistake'*?"

Lukus laughed out loud. "I have a better idea and I think it's gonna help you put your fear of her ever cheating on you again to rest for good. It might be a bit tricky, but I think we can pull it off."

Markus was onboard for any plan Lukus came up with, as long as it accomplished the most important goal of his life.

I'm not resting until Brianna is home and back in our bed where she belongs.

CHAPTER THREE

BRIANNA

*T*wenty-four hours ago, I was making the biggest mistake of my life. If only I could go back and choose not to go with Jake.

Brianna was exhausted, yet she just couldn't get to sleep. Her brain wouldn't shut down the crushing guilt long enough to let sleep claim her. It didn't help that her arms and wrists were uncomfortably tied to the headboard, making it hard to find a comfortable position. At least she wasn't stuck back in the stupid cage she'd slept in the night before.

God, she wanted to call Tiffany. She needed to make amends with her best friend almost as much as Markus. Only Tiffany knew about the dangerous blackmail material her ex held over them both. More importantly, Tiff truly understood the dark part of her psyche that had allowed Jake to keep wedging his way back into her life. In her quiet captivity, Bri swore she'd make her mistakes up to both her husband and her best friend if it was the last thing she did. She just prayed she'd get the chance.

Crushing guilt gripped her as hard as the ropes at her wrists. Sleep eluded her as she obsessed over every horrid detail of the last twenty-four hours. There were so many things she didn't understand, but one truth that was crystal clear was she loved Markus with all her heart. Knowing that, she couldn't reconcile that she'd allowed Jake—the man who had terrorized her and nearly put her in the hospital years before—to blackmail her into a tryst that could ruin her life. It was unforgivable, so how could she expect to be forgiven?

The worst part is he made me come. I may not have enjoyed it, but my body is broken. I hate that I crave the pain.

Worse, as she turned the events around in her head, Brianna remembered Jake was not her only indiscretion in the last twenty-four hours. There was no denying the physical attraction to her husband's best friend.

The freaking gorgeous, sexy... okay, stop Brianna.

Without a doubt, it was Lukus's yummy dominance that was the draw. He'd treated her exactly as she'd dreamed of Markus mastering her. Sure, he'd punished her severely, but she'd deserved every stroke of the paddle, every humiliation he'd dished out. On the surface, Lukus appeared to be the perfect balance of dominance, protectiveness, and tenderness she'd craved all of her adult life. To that end, Bri was smart enough to know she needed to keep her wits about her when he returned.

I wonder what kind of Dom Markus was to Georgie? Was he just like Lukus?

The revelation that Markus had once been part of the D/s lifestyle was fantastical to Bri. As hard as she tried to imagine her husband doing the things to her his best friend had, the memories of his tender lovemaking crowded in, making the vision of him punishing her impossible to see. How could he have hidden his true nature for so long?

A flicker of anger sparked in her heart. Had he lied to her by withholding the truth of his past, or was Lukus right that he'd only hidden his kinks from her to protect her? She'd been determined not to keep secrets about the abuse she'd suffered at Jake's hand, but she instinctively knew her truthfulness at the beginning of their courtship might be the nail in the coffin of their marriage. Before yesterday, she'd just thought Markus wasn't capable of understanding her submissive needs. Now she knew he'd been either too blind, or lazy, to recognize them.

Damn him. Why couldn't he have been more like Lukus who had no trouble ferreting out my deepest secrets—the ones I've never known how to talk about?

Was Lukus with Markus by now? Would he be able to get through to her husband? Would he even try?

The round-robin of endless questions played over in a loop in her brain until she finally fell into an exhausted, dreamless sleep.

———————

Lukus

The men had been bouncing ideas back and forth for about ten minutes when Lukus heard a vibration coming from nearby. They spread out trying to find the source of the noise and Lukus was first to locate Markus's wayward phone.

"Jesus Christ, Markus. At least now I know why you weren't answering your phone. You don't even have the ringer on. It says you've missed four calls from me, one from your office and... for Christ's sake. You've missed six phone calls, two voicemails, and over a dozen text messages from Tiffany. I think she really wants to talk with you."

Markus's face grew dark. "That damn woman lied to me yesterday, too. I feel like I'll never be able to trust her again. It's clear she'll lie for Brianna."

Lukus chuckled at his friend. "Of course, she did. What kind of a real friend wouldn't have lied to you under these circumstances? If it makes you feel any better, Bri told me Tiffany was furious with her yesterday for putting her in that terrible position. I guess Tiffany hates Jake with a passion, and she was furious with Bri for even considering leaving the salon with him."

"I guess that's some consolation, although I'm still pissed. I'm sure Tiff is worried about Bri since she was a no-show at the salon. Not that she would have reached Bri anyway since she left her cell phone in the car last night. Tiff's going to go ballistic when she finds out I know about Jake."

The men headed into the kitchen to grab sandwiches and a cold beer. They spent the next thirty minutes planning how to get Brianna back home where she could be both comforted and punished by her husband and Dom. Markus knew he needed to punish her himself so they could put her infidelity behind them once and for all and start over with a clean slate.

Tiffany phoned two more times while they were in the kitchen. Finally, on the last call, Markus decided it was time to answer. He put the call on speaker so Lukus could hear both sides.

He didn't even answer with a hello. "Tiffany, you need to stop calling me." His voice was hard.

"Oh, thank God you answered. Markus, I think something terrible happened to Brianna. She didn't show up at the salon this morning and she isn't even answering her cell phone. This is so unlike her. I'm really worried." Her voice was shrill with panic.

"You're right about one thing, Tiff. Something really terrible did happen to Brianna. Her husband found out she was fucking around on the side with her ex-boyfriend."

Silence. The men's eyes met as they heard a gulp of air at the other end of the phone. It coincided with the blare of someone's horn. Tiffany was in her car.

Panic had been replaced with pleas. "Oh, no. Markus... you have to..."

"Stop! I don't have to do shit, Tiff. Brianna made her choices and now she's gonna have to live with those choices. You made yours too, didn't you? You flat out lied to me when I called you."

Lukus could hear her crying on the other end of the phone. "Markus, please. I'm so sorry. I wanted to tell you the truth because I'm so worried about Bri. Jake is dangerous. He's hurt her so badly before and it scares the shit out of me."

"I need to go. Stop calling me."

"But, I need—" Markus ended the call before he could hear the rest of her plea.

"Well, you were pretty hard on her considering she wasn't the one who cheated on you." Lukus wasn't sure why, but he was bothered by how that call went down.

"Butt out. Tiffany was our maid-of-honor. She's supposed to be there for us, and our marriage. She should have talked some sense into Brianna instead of covering for her."

"Okay, if you say so. I'm gonna head back to the club—get things set in motion for our plan. You need to seriously take a shower and clean yourself up before you head down. You look like shit man."

"Gee, thanks."

As the men opened the door to head out, Lukus saw an attractive woman jumping out of her car and barreling up the front walkway. The lines of mascara running down the cheeks under her panicked blue eyes told him this must be Tiffany. While Bri's friend focused on confronting Markus, he took a minute to blatantly check the blonde out from head to toe, admiring her long legs, well-rounded ass, and firm tits. Lukus loved how snugly the casual knit, low-cut wrap-around dress she was wearing hugged her curves.

"Markus, I'm so sorry I lied to you. Really, I am, but I need to see Bri right away. You can't keep her from me." Tiffany bravely tried to push past Markus, but he easily stopped her in her tracks. When she continued to try to pass, Lukus moved shoulder to shoulder with Markus, helping to block the entrance to the house. More frustrated, Tiff growled, "I mean it. Let me past so I can go find Bri."

Lukus wanted a closer look into those big blue eyes, so he jumped into the fray. "What makes you think Brianna is even here?"

The look of terror that clouded her wide eyes as Tiffany finally turned to him almost gutted Lukus. "What do you mean? Where else could she be? Oh, my God. Jake didn't hurt her, did he?"

Lukus watched as Tiffany's assertiveness melted with alarm. In that moment, he knew Brianna's fear that her best friend might desert her was completely unfounded. He suspected Tiffany was as loyal as friends came and for some reason, Lukus found himself proud of her for standing up for Brianna in the face of two towering, pissed-off men.

"I think Jake should be the least of your worries," Lukus answered. "Or hers, for that matter."

Tiffany had turned back towards Markus, but his stern response had her finally inspecting Lukus for the first time. He almost chuckled as he saw the range of emotions crossing her expressive face. He fought the urge to reach out to wipe the smeared mascara from her cheeks with the pad of his thumb. The worry lines around her eyes creased as her fear seemed to change to curiosity. "Who are you and what have you done with Brianna?"

"Wouldn't you like to know, baby?"

"Don't *baby* me, asshole. I want to see Bri and I wanna see Bri *now*," she snapped back quickly, actually stomping her foot like a tantrum.

"Or what?" It was impossible to stop from

smiling as he enjoyed toying with the agitated blonde.

"Or… or… damn it… just let me talk to Brianna," she sputtered

Lukus started laughing outright at how flustered Tiffany had become. He fought back the urge to stay and have fun flirting with her. He had a lot of arrangements to make back at the club. "Sorry, sweetheart, but you'll need to stay and duke this out with Markus." He turned to his friend. "Call me when you're headed down, okay?"

"Sure thing. And hey, thanks again." Markus reached out to shake hands with his friend.

"Any time. Turn on your damn phone so I can get through if I need to. Later." With his goodbyes done, he turned to head to his car, but Tiffany had moved to strategically block his departure.

"You aren't going anywhere until you two tell me where Brianna is. I need to know she's safe." She had the look of a mama bear protecting her cub.

Lukus's face broke into a wide grin as he stepped forward, leaving a mere inch between them. He towered over her by nearly six inches in spite of her two-inch heels. He took a minute to drink in the view of her curly, long blonde mane before he instinctively reached out, roughly pulling her against him. He couldn't resist lacing his left hand through her silky hair to grip the back of her neck, tilting her head and forcing her to look up to meet his dominating stare. His right hand wrapped around her lower back, pulling her swiftly into full contact with his rock-hard body. Lukus was almost brought to his knees by the mere scent of her. He found himself mesmerized as he watched her struggling with her emotions as he stared deep into her unique, ocean-blue eyes.

Fuck me. Her body feels like pure sin.

They each stood frozen as they sized each other up. They were strangers. He had no right to manhandle her, yet he clung to her, nonetheless. His cock sprang to life from their bodies being pressed together. It was easy to see that Tiffany was struggling to understand the dynamic between them.

Lukus forced himself to break the silence. "Now, I admire your loyalty to your friend, I really do. But you need to go home now, little girl, before you end up getting yourself hurt. Didn't you know? Bad things can happen to naughty girls who tell lies."

He caught her sharp intake of breath at his blatant threat. He was sure he felt a small quiver race through her body before she looked away in an attempt to break his piercing stare that had her pinned to the spot.

Wiggling to free herself, she begged, "Please... I just need to know Brianna is safe. I'm so worried about her. Please don't let him hurt her again."

Lukus squeezed the back of her neck just hard

enough to regain her attention. "No one is gonna hurt Brianna. Not Jake. Not Markus, and not even me. You're going to have to trust me when I say she's okay. I'll give her the message that you want to talk to her. She'll call as soon as she can."

Tiffany persisted. "Why can't she call me now?"

Lukus's patience was at an end. "You, little girl, need a few lessons in listening and following directions. I've answered your questions. I've reassured you that your friend is safe. You need to simply say *'thank you, Sir'* and let it go."

He paused, giving her a moment to consider his command. "Well?"

Her pupils dilated as she stared at him for several long seconds before finally whispering "Thank you... Sir,"

Lukus broke into a broad grin. "See, that wasn't so hard, and you're welcome." With reluctance, he stepped back, releasing her from his grip. She seemed wobbly on her feet, so he reached out again to hold her steady at the elbow. "Be a good girl and go home now, Tiffany."

He was already moving past her when he heard her almost silent "Yes, Sir." The sound of Tiffany's unprompted submissive response turned him on more than it should have, considering she wasn't a sub at the club.

Damn. I seriously need to find a woman to fuck,

and soon. This hanging out with married people sucks.

Lukus needed to get the hell out of suburbia as soon as possible. He peeled out of Markus's long drive, trying to get his hormones under control as he sped back towards the club.

CHAPTER FOUR

TIFFANY

Tiffany was in an emotional tailspin. She'd feared the worst when Brianna had failed to show up at the salon and had grown panicky when she couldn't reach her. Now that she knew Markus had somehow found out about his wife's infidelity, she was worried about them both. Still, she knew things could be worse.

When she couldn't reach Bri or Markus, she'd called Brianna's parents and brother to see if they'd heard from her. Her first fear was that Jake had abducted her. She shuddered, remembering the nightmares that Brianna's ex was capable of.

Tiffany was so lost in thought she nearly slammed into the back end of the traffic stopped in the middle of the Eisenhower expressway. She had to apply her brakes so hard, her purse and cell phone flew off the front passenger seat and dumped onto the floor, out of reach.

"Shit!"

She swerved to the left so she could keep her eyes on the silver BMW three car-lengths in front of her. She had no idea who the driver—the insanely hot stranger—was, but she had a feeling he knew where Bri was. She'd decided she had a better chance of finding her friend by following the new guy than she did by trying to pry the information out of an angry Markus.

Tiff was furious with herself for how she'd reacted to the mystery man. She'd actually let him intimidate her into acting like a damn submissive. She had no doubt the guy was a Dom. There was no way he couldn't be. He just dripped yummy masculinity and dominance, and while that lethal combination always got her heart racing... and her panties dripping... the bottom line was Tiffany had sworn off the entire D/s lifestyle after seeing what Jake was capable of years before. While she and Brianna had dabbled in the lifestyle, watching her friend terrorized by Jake was enough for Tiff to be scared straight, or more appropriately, scared *vanilla*. The closest Tiffany had gotten to a BDSM relationship since Jake was what she found between the pages of her kinky romance novels.

Still, she couldn't help but compare the few minutes of her interaction with Mr. Tall-Dark-and-Dangerous to last night's date with Jason, the guy she'd been seeing for the last few months. She was fairly certain the two minutes she'd spent in the arms of Markus's friend had had her heart pumping faster than at any time spent in Jason's arms—and that included during sex.

Tiffany had to push her little sedan to try to keep up with the Beamer once they got beyond an accident that had temporarily stalled traffic. She gunned it, knowing she couldn't afford to lose him.

The man seriously drives like a maniac. He's gonna get himself, or someone else, killed.

Tiffany got a sinking feeling in the pit of her stomach when the car she was tailing took an exit several miles west of downtown. Knowing this neighborhood had a bad reputation didn't make her feel any better. She hit her door lock button as she continued her chase, zigzagging north and east, as they edged closer to downtown. She almost lost him more than once and was forced to run two traffic lights to keep up.

She worried that she was following too closely when he unexpectedly turned down a narrow alley between two warehouse-looking brick buildings. He finally stopped and parked close to the end of the building while she pulled to a stop at the end of the alley—as far away as she could while still keeping her eyes on him.

Even from this distance, her breath caught when she got a good look at him as he exited the sports car and headed to a door underneath an awning. He'd had the window down and he stopped to run his hand through his wind-blown shoulder-length dark hair just before using a keycard to gain entry to the building. She could hear the thud of the heavy steel door as it slammed shut behind him.

She waited a few minutes until she felt confident the coast was clear before driving her car up to park directly behind his BMW. Uncertain what she'd expected to find, she needed to investigate if she had a prayer of gaining entry to the building.

The only lettering on the door read *TPP 7969*. Of course, her attempt to open the door was met with resistance. She saw a keypad along with the keycard reader and spent a few minutes trying to guess the code.

She was about to get back in her car to drive around the building in hopes of finding another entrance when someone grabbed her from behind. Her attacker's arms wrapped completely around her torso, trapping her arms at her sides and holding her back immobile against a rock-hard chest.

The girls had taken self-defense classes over the years. She was happy when her training kicked in, remembering to lift her high-heeled foot and stomp down on her attacker's foot as hard as possible. This might have been an effective strategy had it met with any other pair of shoes in the city. Unfortunately, just her luck, her attacker was wearing steel-toed boots. All Tiffany managed to do was twist her ankle from the force of her failed defensive move.

"Ouch! Shit that hurts. Goddamn it, let me go! I'm going to call the police! Let me go!" She screamed, floundering to get free while trying to get someone to call for help. But she was in a sketchy part of town, down a deserted alley, and despite her attempts to wiggle free, her captor was just too strong. She fought like a she-cat until she finally ran out of strength, slumping against the muscular body behind her.

"Shhh. You need to settle down now, baby." His voice was low, but demanding as he held her up.

Oh, my God! It's him.

He answered almost as if he'd heard her thoughts. "I know... I'm like a bad penny. I just keep turning up."

He didn't release her. Instead, Markus's friend buried his face in her curls. He took a deep breath, drawing in the scent of her hair. His lips brushed across her ear as he softly chastised her. "You don't listen very well, do you? I distinctly remember telling you to go home and wait there for Brianna to call, yet here you are."

A strange combination of relief and trepidation invaded her thoughts. An odd premonition warned her he might be more dangerous than some random hoodlum. She refused to show her fear.

"Let go of me and take me to Brianna. I know

she's here." Tiffany tried to fling free of him, but his grip was too hard.

"Do you now? And what makes you think that?"

"Just the way you and Markus were talking. What is this place, anyway?"

Tiff could feel the outline of his hardening cock pressing into the small of her back. She should be pissed that she could feel him slowly grinding his hips to increase the friction between their bodies. Traitorous juices spilled into her panties. She needed to put some space between them if she had a hope of not embarrassing herself.

"I'm serious. You need to let go of me now."

Without warning, he abruptly released her. Only too late did Tiffany realize just how injured her right ankle was from her earlier, failed defensive move. Without his stabilizing arms holding her up, she immediately toppled over when her injured ankle gave out on her. Only his fast reflexes stopped her from face-planting onto the dirty alley.

"Whoa there." He tried to hold her again as she flailed around ungracefully.

Tiffany lifted her right leg to take her weight off of her pained ankle. She hopped around, trying to catch her balance until she found herself once again in his tight embrace–this time face to face. Was that concern in his green eyes?

She finally found her voice. "Thanks for catching me before I ended up on the ground."

He held her steady while looking down at her feet. "How's your ankle? Do you think you can walk on it?"

"I just need a few minutes. I'm sure it'll be fine." Tiffany grimaced in pain as she attempted to put some weight on her injury, trying to evaluate how serious it was.

"So where are we and what does TPP stand for?" she asked as she tried to hobble on her sore ankle.

He chuckled mysteriously. "I'm not so sure you want to know the answer to that question, little girl. You know what they say—I could tell you, but then I'd have to kill you."

His answer annoyed her. "Fine, then maybe we should start with something easier, like who the hell are you?"

The mystery man looked amused at her sassy response.

He waited long enough to answer that Tiff was beginning to think he was ignoring her.

"My name is Lukus Mitchell. I'm Markus's best friend and old roommate from college. I own this building. It's where my security firm is headquartered. It's also where I live." If that were true, having known Markus for three years, Tiffany was shocked that she hadn't met him before. And she was certain they hadn't met, because she would have definitely remembered meeting Lukus Mitchell if their paths had crossed before.

He paused, moving his left hand up to run through her curls before gripping her tightly behind the neck, just like he had done at Markus's house. Tiffany's breath caught at the glare of confidence Lukus emanated, their faces just inches apart.

"You sure you want to know what TPP stands for, baby? I'll help you to your car right now. I'll let you drive away. But, if I tell you what TPP stands for, you're committing to coming inside. Sure... you'll get to see Brianna, but you'll also be agreeing to follow the same rules that she's following as my... *guest.*"

Tiffany's instincts screamed for her to turn around and drive away. She sensed she was in over her head with this bossy man, but she was the submissive moth to his dominant flame. She didn't want to leave him... yet. And more importantly, she wasn't going to leave without seeing Brianna.

"You're crazy if you think I'm leaving Brianna here alone with you. I demand you take me to her right now." Her tone displayed far more confidence than she felt. It took all her self-control to keep looking him in the eye, refusing to look away.

Lukus exhaled, clearly frustrated with her pushing him. "Okay, little girl. I don't want you to say later that I didn't warn you. Remember, you're going in by choice. I also want you to remember that so far today you've disobeyed me twice by not going home when ordered. You put yourself in danger when you ran through at least three red lights trying to keep up with me. And finally, you blatantly lied to my best friend about something as important as his wife's safety and fidelity. Tiffany, you've been a very naughty girl."

Who the hell talked like this to someone he barely knew? Her heart pounded in her chest so hard and fast, she was starting to feel woozy. Her brain was once again demanding she jump in her car and get the hell out of there. Instead she simply whispered, "What does TPP stand for, Lukus?"

The glare of his hard gaze only made his answer more terrifying. "It stands for The Punishment Pit. It's where Dominants bring their naughty submissives to be severely punished. It looks like you've come to the right place since we've already established you've been a bad girl."

Tiffany was seriously in danger of toppling over from the shock of his words.

Without warning, Lukus stooped down to lift her, sprained ankle and all, over his shoulder in a fireman's hold. He wasted no time in swiping his card and opening the door to the club. Tiffany made an attempt at flailing, but only until he brought his free hand up to smack her hard on her upturned ass.

Her cry echoed through the alley, but no one was there to hear her.

CHAPTER FIVE

B rianna awoke disoriented. The sound of something crashing in the next room had startled her from her much-needed sleep. She wiggled her hands against the restraints as she scanned the room.

"Hello. Is someone there? Lukus, is that you?"

When silence greeted her, she suspected she simply dreamed the loud bang. Bri closed her eyes, hoping to recapture the oblivion that would temporarily shield her from her obsessive fears and regrets.

Another sound... softer... closer. She glanced to the doorway just in time to catch a motion out of the corner of her eye. This time she knew she hadn't imagined it. Lying naked and restrained, she scanned the area nervously.

"Who's there? Lukus?"

Brianna trained her gaze on the bedroom door.

After a few long seconds, she was rewarded with the glimpse of a woman trying to sneak a peek into the room undetected. The dark-haired beauty jerked back quickly when their eyes met, but the jig was up.

Brianna tried to coax her out.

"Please," she implored softly. "Can you come untie me? I need to go to the bathroom."

Bri would try anything to get her aching arms free, even if only for a few minutes. Not to mention, the ropes wrapped around her breasts felt more uncomfortable now that she was awake. Bri wasn't used to the constricted feeling that was not entirely unpleasant. The constant pressure of the rope was like an invisible tie to Lukus—a reminder of the power he yielded, even when absent.

She tried again to convince the visitor. "Hey, I know you're there. There's no point in hiding now."

A petite young woman took a few hesitant steps into the room, hovering near the door. Her eyes were wide—frightened—as if Brianna was somehow going to hurt her. The newcomer remained silent as she evaluated Brianna's predicament.

It took a few minutes, but Brianna finally recognized the brunette as the slave girl from the dungeon the night before. She'd been naked and weary looking on stage. Today, she looked young, fresh, and almost innocent, dressed in a flared floral mini skirt paired with a long-sleeved lavender sweater cut low enough to emphasize her ample cleavage. The low neckline also put her thick gold choker on display.

There was no mistaking it was a submissive's collar. An unwanted and completely unjustified feeling of jealously flared up in Brianna as she wondered if this was Lukus's collared slave. Still, there was no denying she must belong to Lukus since she was here in his home. She thought back to the night before, when both Lukus and Derek had used the girl's ponytail as a handle while face-fucking her. Today, her beautiful hair was flowing around her shoulders and down her back.

"Hi. My name is Brianna. I saw you last night downstairs with Lukus and Derek. What's your name?"

The girl's wide eyes got impossibly bigger at Brianna's comment. She opened her mouth as if to talk, but then closed it again. It was clear she was struggling to keep quiet. When she finally answered, her authoritative tone was unexpected.

"You shouldn't call them Lukus and Derek. They're Master Lukus and Master Derek or just plain Sirs. It's not right for a sub to be so informal," she scolded.

"Well, it should be okay since I'm not their submissive. I'm..." Bri's voice trailed off, unsure how to explain her relationship with the men since she had no clue herself. She simply ended with, "I'm married to Lukus's best friend."

"I know," the girl spat. "I can't believe you'd be stupid enough to cheat on Master Markus." As soon as the words were spoken, the girl clamped her hand over her mouth, turning to rush back out.

Ignoring the obvious insult, Bri shouted at her. "Wait a minute! Don't go! You know Markus?"

The visitor froze in the doorway, still refusing to talk. Bri tried again to befriend her. "I'm sorry. I still didn't catch your name," Bri urged more gently.

No answer. Her eyes darted between Brianna and the door, conflicted with her decision. Brianna had just about given up hope when the pretty woman lowered her hand still across her mouth and answered Bri's question.

"I'm Rachel," she confided. "I'm Master Derek's submissive and collared slave. I've also been his wife for the last four years."

Brianna hated the misplaced sense of relief at Rachel's introduction. But that relief quickly turned to curiosity when she realized Rachel most likely had information about Markus's hidden past life.

"Nice to meet you, Rachel," Brianna said, keeping her tone conversational and non-threatening. "Four years is a long time. You must have known Markus back when he was coming to the club before he met me, right?"

Brianna's heart raced, unsure what answers she was hoping for. She was desperate for information about the secrets her husband had been keeping from her. She should probably feel guilty for misleading her new friend, but that didn't stop her from fishing. "You know, back when he and Georgie used to come here."

Rachel looked relieved. "Oh, so you know about Georgie? I didn't want to be the one to tell you about him bringing someone else here."

"Well, sure. I mean, I know about his first wife. I'm sure there are details he might not have told me about her because he was trying to protect me, but I know they belonged to the club." This seemed like a logical enough guess for Bri to put out there in hopes of drawing more information out about her husband.

Rachel's eyes looked to be getting a little dewy. "I hated that Master Markus stopped coming to the club. It really upset Master Lukus, especially at first. He tried to hide it, but Master Derek and I could see how hurt and alone he was back then. The only good thing that came out of the Sirs' arrest was we got to finally see Master Markus again when he'd come by to work on the case."

That was a startling new piece of intelligence. "Yes, he came by here quite a bit, didn't he?" Brianna kept probing for details, despite a growing trepidation of what secrets she might uncover.

"Well sure, but it was almost always in the middle of the day instead of at night like he used to. We would sometimes go to his office downtown or meet at a restaurant for lunch. He sure has a beautiful view of the river from his office."

"Yes... yes he does."

Brianna wasn't sure how she felt about this beautiful submissive visiting her husband at work or going out to lunch with him, but surely Derek and Lukus had been there too. And thankfully Markus had been at the club during business hours instead of visiting at night as a Dom. It was heartbreaking enough to discover that he'd been withholding his dominant nature from her; if he'd been going behind her back to go to The Punishment Pit to *play* with other subs... well, that would just push her over the edge.

"Rachel, can you please undo my arms just long enough for me to run to the bathroom? I promise, I won't do anything stupid and I'll come right back so you can tie me up again. Master Lukus doesn't even need to know."

Terror painted Rachel's face. "Oh, I don't think so. Master Derek told me not to even talk to you so I'm already in so much trouble. I know he wouldn't want me to untie you." She started to turn to leave.

"Oh please... I promise I'll be fast. I really need your help, Rachel."

Brianna saw the indecision on Rachel's face as she turned and with great hesitancy untied the ropes binding Brianna to the headboard. Once free of the bindings, Brianna took a minute to rub her wrists and was just about to sit up when Lukus burst into the room.

"What the fuck is going on here, Rachel?"

Lukus voice boomed, clearly pissed. Brianna's view of the angry Master was blocked, but she had a front row seat to watching Rachel's panic, immediately kneeling to apologize.

"I'm so sorry," she whimpered. "Please forgive me."

Now that Rachel had dropped to her knees, Brianna got a good look at Lukus. Under any other circumstances, she would have been focused on his anger. But it was the woman thrown over his left shoulder in a fireman's hold who got Brianna's attention.

"Tiffany! Is that you?"

"Yes, it's me," Tiffany answered, her words muffled by her graceless position. "So glad you can recognize me just from the view of my ass up in the air, swung over this damn barbarian's shoulder. Lukus! Put me down!"

Tiff struggled to be free of his tight hold. Her friend was ineffectually pelting his back with her fists. Rather than release her, Lukus instead swatted her ass several times, hard, with his open palm. She squealed, but it did stop her flailing.

Lukus looked to Bri as if he were about to self-combust and really... who the hell would blame him? He was a dominant Master who found himself faced with not one, but *three* defiant women. She was tempted to giggle at his obvious distress, but luckily thought better of it.

Knowing how he felt about having Brianna here in his private loft, she could only assume with Tiffany here, he'd had an interesting afternoon. Unsurprisingly, he decided to address his easiest problem first.

"I'm very disappointed in you Rachel," he said, fixing her with a withering gaze. "Did Master Derek give you instructions when he sent you up here?"

"Yes Sir, he did," she managed to squeak out without looking up at Master Lukus.

"And those instructions were what exactly?"

"I was supposed to just come and make sure nothing bad happened to Master Markus's wife until you returned, Sir."

"And... were those his only instructions to you?"

"No, Sir." Rachel began to whimper.

"I'm waiting, Rachel, and you know I don't like to wait. What were his complete instructions to you?"

Brianna had trouble hearing her, she was talking so softly. "I was to be quiet and not even let her know I was here. I wasn't supposed to talk to her unless the building was on fire, Sir."

"And yet I arrive and you're not only very visible, but you've managed to free her from the ropes I secured her in *and* you're carrying on like you're best friends having a damn slumber party. Since the building is clearly not on fire, what am I missing here?"

Brianna had to hand it to the guy. He was uber scary when he turned on his Dom. Still, she couldn't let Rachel take the blame.

Clutching the sheets around her nakedness as she sat up, Brianna jumped in out of sheer guilt. "Lukus, stop yelling at her. This is my fault. I heard her moving around and kept calling until she finally came in. She didn't want to talk or let me loose, but I made her. Don't be mad at Rachel."

Lukus moved closer to the bed and the subjugated slave on the floor, his face turning red. "Nice of you to offer an explanation, Brianna. I'll see you get equal punishment as well for your part in this debacle. But that changes nothing. Rachel is not a newbie submissive. She knows the rules and she knows what happens when she chooses to disobey her Master's orders, don't you Rachel?"

"Yes, Sir." She answered softly, resigned to her fate. "I'm so sorry, Master Lukus."

"I'm sure you are. I want you to go down to the dungeon. Get undressed and drape yourself over the spanking bench and wait for me there. I'll be down later to carry out your punishment of a dozen lashes with the cane for your blatant disobedience today."

Rachel's gasp told Brianna this was a severe punishment for the young submissive. Then it hit her. That meant *she* was going to get a dozen lashes with the cane. Her heart pounded at the thought of it.

When Rachel didn't immediately follow directions, Lukus raised his voice. "What are you waiting for? Were my instructions unclear?"

Rachel was now sitting straight up on the floor, kneeling in front of Master Lukus. "It's just that Master Derek is going to be so very angry at me. Do you need to tell him about this, Sir?"

"What do you think?" Lukus spat.

"I think you're going to tell him, Sir."

"You're damn straight I'm gonna tell him. He needs to know his wife and submissive disobeyed his direct order."

Brianna could hear Rachel crying softly. "I understand, Sir. It's just he believes if I get in trouble with you for something, then it must be really bad and so I'll receive double the punishment from him. That means I'll be getting thirty-six lashes with the cane, Sir."

It was Brianna's turn to gasp. That was barbaric, and it was all her fault.

For the briefest second, Bri saw indecision on Lukus's face before his Dom mask hardened. "I guess you should have thought of the consequences before you blatantly defied direct orders. I'm pretty sure this punishment will be a memorable one for you and therefore I suspect you'll be following directions in the future, won't you?"

"Oh yes, Sir."

Lukus's voice softened when he gave his final order to Rachel. "Get up and go now, Rachel. Do as I say. Prepare yourself for your punishment. While you're waiting for me, I want you to think about why you're being punished, do you understand?"

"Yes, Sir. Thank you, Sir."

Rachel scrambled to her feet and rushed out of the room without a backward glance. Lukus and Brianna were locked in a stare-down as she sent him daggers for how he treated Rachel. "I told you. This wasn't her fault. Why did you have to treat her like that?"

"Let's get something straight here, sweetheart. This is a punishment club. Rachel is a full-time, collared submissive who chooses to live her life by the rules we've set out for her. She broke those rules and as a result, she not only expects to be punished, but she'll be disappointed if I don't punish her. It's how things work around here."

"So, you just punish people, even when they do nothing wrong? That's bullshit!"

"Enough. I'm not gonna discuss this with you. This just proves what I was telling you earlier. You obviously have zero real experience as a sub regardless of what that Dom wanna-be, Jake, thought he was teaching you. Any submissive with an ounce of training would know not to talk back right now."

"Oh, really. I think that's exactly what I'm doing, Lukus. You need to—"

Their argument was interrupted by Tiffany's muffled interjection from behind Lukus's back. "Excuse me. Can the two of you stop fighting long enough to please put me down? I'm starting to lose feeling in my feet and hands from being upside down for so long."

Lukus rolled his eyes, clearly losing his patience with all of the women determined to ruin his Saturday. Walking to the bed, he unceremoniously dumped Tiffany from his shoulder to land with a bounce on the soft, king-sized bed. The women wasted no time rushing to hug the other, each holding on for dear life.

"Oh, thank God you're okay, Bri. I was so worried about you when you didn't show up at the salon this morning and then I couldn't reach you on your cell. I thought sure Jake had abducted you and carried you back out to the cabin to finish you off."

Brianna was alarmed at the thought, but relieved her friend cared enough to try and find her. "I'm fine, Tiff... well as fine as I can be, all things considered. I'm so damn sorry I got you dragged into this whole mess."

Tiffany was part laughing, part tearing up as she held onto her friend. "You should be sorry! Not only did you scare me half to death, but I've been screamed at and treated like shit by your husband. Then I almost died on the Eisenhower trying to keep up with Mr. Speed-Demon over there." She paused to shake her thumb in Lukus's direction. "Next, I sprained my ankle trying to defend myself from a would-be attacker in the alley. My limbs are numb. It's like I've fallen down some rabbit hole into this ... BDSM Neverland and worst of all? I'm sitting here hugging my *naked* best friend while she mashes her tied-up boobs into me. I didn't think we were this kind of friends, Bri."

Brianna heard a rare chuckle from Lukus. Glancing at him as she held her cheek against Tiffany's shoulder, she confirmed genuine amusement shining in Lukus's eyes; a rare smile lighting up his face.

When their eyes met, Brianna mouthed the silent words '*thank you*' to him. If anything, his smile got brighter before he turned and left the bedroom, closing the door quietly behind him.

After watching him leave, Brianna pulled back to get a good look at her best friend. "Tiff, you're the best friend a girl could ever ask for. I'm so glad you're here. I have so much to tell you, but first, tell me more about how Markus looked when you saw him."

CHAPTER SIX

LUKUS

Lukus closed the door, shaking his head as the two women clung to each other chatting a mile a minute. He decided he was in desperate need of a drink.

*Figures. I have two of the finest women I've ever had in my bed, together at the same time, and I **still** can't get laid. I seriously need to find someone to fuck and soon.*

Lukus wasted no time in pouring himself a whiskey. He shouldn't be drinking. He already felt more out of control than he had in years. He wasn't sure why his friends' problems should be impacting his life so much, but without a doubt, Brianna's infidelity had triggered events that had him struggling to maintain his perspective.

After knocking back a quick shot, Lukus sunk into his favorite chair and looked out over the Chicago skyline. It was late afternoon, one of his favorite times of the day to take in the busy city as the sun reflected off the distant lake and tall skyscrapers. Lukus allowed the view to calm him as he sorted out what he had to do next. He couldn't afford to turn into an emotional pussy over a few wayward women who, if all went as planned, would be out of his hair for good by midnight.

Digging into his pocket, he pulled out his phone and called Derek.

"Hey, glad you finally made it back."

"Yeah. I got back a few minutes ago. For the record, this day really blows."

"What now? Did Markus kick your ass for wanting to screw his wife?"

"He wanted to at first, but I managed to defuse the situation. You still in the security office?"

"Yeah."

"I think you'd better come up. We have a lot to talk about."

"That doesn't sound good. Maybe I'll stay down here." Derek tried to laugh before Lukus cut him off.

"Just come up, will ya? I'm so fucking sick of everyone arguing with me today."

"Screw you, man." Derek hung up on his friend.

Lukus barely had time to get up and pour two shots of whiskey before he heard the elevator arriving at the loft. Derek strolled in. He had a scowl on his face until he saw Lukus holding out the shot glass like an olive branch.

"Alright," Lukus said apologetically. "I'm not going get all mushy, but I'm sorry I'm taking my shitty day out on you."

Derek reached out to grab the shot, downing it before he answered his friend. "Don't sweat it, man. It'll take a bit more than your piss-poor mood to hurt my feelings. I'm not one of the submissives."

"Thank fuck for that. We have more than enough of those around here."

Plopping down in Lukus's favorite chair, Derek responded. "I don't think you're upset we have too many submissives around here."

Moving to sit on the nearby couch instead, Lukus retorted, "Oh really. And just what do you think has me all upset, Dr. Parker?"

Derek just grinned. "Touché. I'm just saying I think your biggest problem is that we seem to have a boatload of women around here who *aren't* submissive, at least not submissive enough to behave. I saw your little encounter in the alley on the security cameras. Who's the good-looking blonde you hoisted over your shoulder and carried in like a caveman?"

Lukus shot an annoyed look at his friend before answering. "She's Brianna's best friend, Tiffany. You know, the one who works at the salon with her. She's also the woman who flat-out lied to Markus yesterday to protect Brianna."

"Oh, yeah. I thought she looked familiar. I remember thinking she looked like a hot piece of ass when we were doing the surveillance on the salon a few months ago."

"Yeah, well it's just what we need. Another damn married woman hanging around. It'll be just my luck to have her fucking husband show up here next, making a big stink and wanting to know what the hell I did with his wife."

"What are you talking about? She's not married. In fact, she'd just started dating some guy when we were doing background checks. I don't remember his name. We checked him out though in case he was involved with Brianna and he came back clean. He's some boring business type. Jeremy... Jack... John. Some 'J' name."

Lukus tried to school his reaction to the news, but his mind raced, replaying the last hour over in his head as he tried to figure out what had made him believe Tiffany was married. He'd just assumed someone that beautiful had to be someone's trophy wife.

Excellent investigative work there, Mitchell. Still, it doesn't change a thing. She's not a submissive. Not really. She's off-limits.

It was clear his dick hadn't gotten that last message. Just knowing she was single was like the starter's shot at a race. His erection grew uncomfortable in his jeans as he remembered the feel of Tiffany's curvy body pressed against him, and her unsolicited, submissive "Yes, Sir." Lukus shifted in his seat, rearranging his family jewels in an attempt to relieve his discomfort.

"Earth to Lukus. Aw shit. I see it in your eyes. You're thinking about fucking *her* now, aren't you? Well, before you do, keep in mind she's not a club member and as the recently acquitted, minority owner of this club, may I remind you of the dangers we both face if you so much as touch her in a way that might be seen in court as abuse? It doesn't make a damn bit of difference that she's up here in your loft and not down in the club. She's on club property so you keep your twitching spanking hand and frustrated cock to yourself, you hear me? I'd like to at least enjoy our last acquittal for a few days before we get slapped with the next lawsuit, if it's all the same to you."

Lukus knew Derek was right. It would be insane to do what he really wanted to do, which was march into his bedroom and show Tiffany what a real Dom thought of her naughty ways. He also knew full well he needed to calm down and get his emotions in check because in the condition he was in right now, he'd risk taking things too far.

"Don't worry man. My body may want to burst in there and fuck 'em both, but my brain is still in control. I'm not as stupid as you seem to think I am."

"You're not stupid, Lukus. You're completely justified to feel all the shit you're feeling. I know the last few years have been hard on you. I've seen you changing. There was a time I thought you'd be happy being the Master of Many forever. Not anymore. You can deny it all you want, but you just aren't enjoying being here at the club punishing other people's subs day-in and day-out anymore. It's turning into just a job for you, and I know your heart isn't in it like it used to be. I started to notice it after the shit with Markus blew up a few years ago and it's gotten worse since the lawsuit. I've been wanting to talk to you about it for a few months and told myself I'd wait until after the shit with the trial died down. Now all this other crap with Brianna has blown up and it just seems like a sign."

"A sign of what? Who the hell are you now—Dr. Phil? I think you need to stop trying to psychoanalyze me and worry about your own submissive instead. Just wait till you hear what your wife did today."

"Don't try to change the subject. I want to hear everything about Rachel, but there's something else I've been holding back from telling you because I wasn't sure how you'd take the news and honestly, I needed a few weeks to get my own head wrapped around it myself."

Lukus didn't miss the mixed look of panic and excitement on Derek's face. "What? You win the lottery? You and Rachel running away from home?"

Derek broke into a broad grin. "Better."

His partner certainly had his full attention. "Better, you say? Well, that must be some news then. Why do I feel a headache coming on?"

"I won't blame you if you go ballistic on me man, but I've been bursting to tell you and forced myself to wait until after the trial because you had enough shit to worry about."

Lukus saw him take a deep breath and could tell Derek was nervous, which was very curious. Derek was *never* nervous.

"Rachel is almost three months pregnant. Can you believe my sorry ass is gonna be a father? I'm probably gonna have the poor kid screwed up before it can walk."

Derek's face had lit up like a Christmas tree, he looked so elated. Lukus wasn't sure why, but the unexpected news hit him hard. For the briefest of moments his stomach churned, and he felt like he might throw up. He recovered enough to speak. "Wow. That's a fucking surprise. I didn't even know you two were interested in starting a family."

He hadn't been shocked at all when James and Mary had settled down and started having kids. When Markus had turned in his Dom card to settle down in suburbia with Brianna, he was sure they'd be popping out babies soon. But not in a million years did he ever see Derek and Rachel ever having children.

Even though Derek and Rachel were married, they'd always lived a 24/7 D/s relationship with heavy age-play tendencies. It wasn't exactly the kind of relationship that lended itself to raising kids. Lukus tried to imagine Rachel walking around their house naked, like she usually did with only her collar, wrist, and ankle cuffs as accessories. When she did wear outfits, they were baby clothes and diapers. How was that going to work when she had to care for a real baby, or even worse, years later when the kid was older? Would Rachel still sit naked at Derek's feet at the dinner table, her ass striped with belt marks from her last discipline session?

It's not going to work. Rachel is going to change. How can she not? It will be impossible to be a good full-time sub and a good mother at the same time.

Of all his friends, Lukus had been sure Derek would never want to trade in his whip and spanking paddle for diapers and bottles, but clearly he'd been wrong. An unwelcome and fresh wave of jealousy hit Lukus as he added Derek to his list of close friends who were now lucky enough to have it all.

"I'm happy for you, man," Lukus finally said, and despite his jealousy, he meant it. "I can tell you're excited and while I have my doubts about how your hard-ass detective and Dom skills are going to translate into fatherhood, I'm still thrilled for you and Rachel."

"Thanks, man. I'm not really sure about it myself, but I know it's important to Rach. Her sisters all have a bunch of kids and while she was never too pushy about it, I knew before we got married she wasn't going to be happy unless we had some too. When I asked her what she wanted for her birthday, she said all she really wanted was to go off the pill."

"Well hell, her birthday was barely four months ago."

Derek grinned from ear to ear. "I guess I have some good little swimmers."

Lukus laughed at his friend. "Well of course you do. They must be Doms too. They got in there and took control, although it probably doesn't hurt that you two fuck like rabbits. I'm not sure what to say other than congratulations man, really." Only then did Lukus remember where Rachel was right at the moment. "I wonder if this means I need to change my planned punishment for the mother of your unborn child. She really pissed me off today."

"Rachel? Not her too? Where is she, anyway?"

Lukus took a few minutes to fill his partner in on his wife's mischief. Derek's complexion grew redder by the minute.

Lukus wrapped up, "Can you believe it? It's so unlike her. I already sentenced her to a dozen lashes with the cane, but now that I know she's pregnant, I'll let you handle this any way you think is best. She can't get away without some punishment though."

Derek grimaced. "Fuck. I'm so sorry man. I

never dreamed she'd disobey me so blatantly. No. You need to punish her. I've already had this discussion with her. She is and will always be my submissive. Sure, once the kid comes we'll have to make adjustments to what we do in public verses what we have to do in private, but it doesn't matter. She earned the cane and she knows this means she'll be getting double that from me too."

"I don't know... " Lukus didn't like the severity of the punishment in light of the new news.

Derek tried to alleviate his fears. "I've been doing a ton of research and really, we don't have to worry too much about hurting the baby, at least not until the third trimester. We've never been into the really dangerous shit anyway and we just need to watch her reaction more carefully and maybe break up big punishments into smaller chunks."

"If you're sure, man. I want you there just to keep an extra eye on her. We need to keep her safe more now than ever. Before we go down to take care of Rachel, I want to go over the idea that Markus and I came up with today. We have a plan that's hopefully going to get Brianna properly punished and home where she belongs tonight."

"You must have gotten through to him after all then."

"I think I did. Markus really doesn't want the plan carried out with a big audience though, and I honestly don't blame him. They have so much shit to work through and who knows how this is going to go. I want to close the whole club down tonight. Can we get the word out to all the members that we'll be closed for one night? I know it's late notice."

"That seems a bit extreme, not to mention expensive. Saturday nights are our best nights, and we're gonna really piss some Doms off with the late notice. You sure you want to do this?"

Standing, Lukus looked at his friend. "Yeah, I'm sure. We owe it to Markus to handle this privately. Let's head down to the club office. We can send out emails and texts to everyone. I'll explain the plan to you on the way since I'll need your help for a bit of it. I think you're really going to like it."

"I'm sure I will. Your punishment plans are always... *interesting*. I feel a really big hard-on coming."

"Welcome to my world. I've been ready to fucking explode for the last twenty-four hours. At least you have Rachel for stress relief. I'm gonna keel over from blue balls if I don't get laid soon."

"I don't feel too sorry for you, Lukus. You could call a dozen subs from your contact list and eleven would be here, naked and kneeling, within the hour. If you aren't getting any, it's because you're just getting too damn picky."

Lukus didn't bother answering his friend because he knew he was right. He could have had a harem of subs here in no time. Subs who would do anything and everything he asked of them. They would behave like proper submissives and follow directions to a T. They wouldn't talk back. They wouldn't sass or argue. They wouldn't push him away or tell him he had to stop. Yep, Derek was right. He could get laid a dozen times by a dozen different women before midnight if he really wanted. The problem was—he didn't want that, not anymore. He wasn't sure exactly when, but somewhere along the way he'd started wanting something different, something more.

Yep… I'm still so fucked.

CHAPTER SEVEN

BRIANNA

"So, let me get this straight. Lukus was at my house and Markus was there and they looked all chummy?"

Tiff sighed, telling Bri she was losing her patience. "Yes, for the third time, yes. Lukus was just coming out of your house when I got there."

Brianna couldn't help but keep pumping her friend for information. She was desperate to see her husband. "Tell me again. What did Markus look like? Did he look like he was going to forgive me?"

"Bri, I told you. Markus was a total dick to me. He treated me like *I* was the one who had cheated on him. He looked like complete shit. I've never seen him appear anything close to as disheveled. He had on crumpled clothes that had crap all spilled down the front. He hadn't showered or shaved. His hair was all matted and messy. And before you ask again... no... I didn't see any other women there, because like I said, the men didn't let me get past the front door. I love Markus to death, but even I would've made him shower before I let him touch me looking and smelling like he did. If he did have a woman there, she'd have to have been a total skank to want him like that."

"Oh, gee. Thanks Tiff. I feel so much better now." Bri let her sarcasm come through loud and clear.

"Any time. What are friends for?" Tiff grinned from ear to ear, helping Bri relax slightly as her friend questioned her back. "I just can't believe Markus is really a Dom and he used to belong to the punishment club. Are you sure Lukus isn't just trying to pull one over on you?"

"Pretty sure, yeah. And honestly, the more I think about it, the more I believe it. You should see him in court. He's all alpha-male. I've never been able to figure out how he could just switch it off when he came home at night. Seeing him and Lukus together last night and then finding out James is a Dom, too... well, I just believe Markus can be a Dom like Lukus and James. Rachel even confirmed it for me. She knew Markus when he and Georgie used to come here. I'm just so damn mad at him for hiding it from me."

Tiff nodded. "You know. Now that I think about it, watching the two men together today at your house, I guess I can believe it, too. If Markus is even half as good of a Dom as Lukus, I think you're finally gonna get the kind of marriage you've been wanting all of these years, Bri."

Doubt threatened to drown her optimism. "Well, that's if he can forgive me for the biggest mistake of my life. Let's not forget he's still trying to get me to sign the quickie divorce papers."

Tiffany used a few seconds of silence to glance around the room, showing interest in a line of pictures on the dresser across the room.

Bri kept going with her train of thoughts. "But I'm more opposed than ever to signing. I'm never gonna give up on getting him back—I love him— but, especially if there's a chance he can be everything I ever needed." That's when Brianna paused, her eyes connecting with her BFF. "Wait... how exactly do you know how good of a Dom Lukus is? Did you... I mean did he...?"

"What?" Tiffany's eyebrow flew up. "Are you crazy? We just met! The damn brute did grab me though. He even held me immobile while he lectured me about how naughty it was to lie for you and then how I needed to be a good girl and just go home. I should've slapped his face, but instead he somehow tricked me into saying 'Yes, Sir' and 'No, Sir' like I was one of his damn submissives. He just caught me at a weak moment. I'm ready for him now. If he thinks he's gonna order me around like a submissive, he has another thing coming. I took that self-defense class. I'll kick him in the balls like my instructor taught me."

"Yeah, right. Good luck with that." Brianna giggled at the mental image. "I'd pay to see you take down Lukus."

"I'm serious. He's in for a shock if he thinks he's gonna keep manhandling me like he has so far. I'll call Jason and have him come down here to pick me up and if Lukus tries anything, I'll have Jason take him out."

That did it. Brianna couldn't contain herself at her friend's ludicrous idea. She started giggling harder, much to her best friend's angst. "Jason? You think Jason could last thirty seconds against Lukus? Seriously Tiff, I don't know what you see in that guy. He's cute in a sort of feminine way, but you'll get him killed if you call him down here to save you. Every jury in the country would convict you as an accomplice for sending him to his certain death."

"Stop being so mean. You're totally exaggerating."

Bri noticed Tiffany wasn't arguing very strenuously. Sometimes she thought she knew her best friend better than Tiff knew herself. She only had to keep staring at her, waiting patiently, until Tiff finally broke down. "Okay, okay. So, he's a total wimp. I truly think he spends more time and money on primping than I do, and that's saying something. Last weekend I asked him to help me hang that new artwork I got at the gallery opening you and I went to last month, and he actually refused to help, saying he couldn't use a hammer and didn't want to mess up his recent manicure. He sat his ass on my couch and watched me hang it all by myself, and when I almost fell off the chair, he didn't even come and help keep me steady. He just sat there and called me a klutz. Who am I kidding? I should have kicked him to the curb that very minute."

"I rest my case. The guy is a total dishrag. I know Jake managed to scare the shit out of both of us, but Tiff... I know you'll never really be happy with a guy like Jason. You won't admit it, but you want a dominant man, a strong, protective man like Lukus or Markus just as much as I do."

"What, and you think I'd be better off with a Dom who bosses me around and expects me to be a mindless toy to play with? You've read too many romance novels, Bri. Men like that don't exist outside of books. You keep wanting to have it all. But we either get a Jason or a Jake and no offense, but I've seen enough of Jake to pass on that."

"You're wrong, Tiff. I refuse to believe that. There are all different levels in between the extremes. Markus isn't like Jake or Jason. He's perfect."

"Lucky you. So, you found the one-in-a-million. The rest of us have to take one extreme or the other."

"Oh really... and what about Lukus? He isn't like Jake or Jason either. He's perfect, too."

Tiffany scoffed at her friend. "Perfect for who? You've known the guy for less than twenty-four hours and if I heard you right, in those twenty-four hours he's tied you up, whipped you, paddled you, tied you in ropes, made you sleep in a cage, and even forced you to have a punishment enema, for God's sake. Thanks, but no thanks. I can pass on that."

"Don't forget he also made me come more times than I can count without even having sex with me." Brianna lowered her voice to a conspiratorial whisper. "Just think what he could do if he was really trying."

Bri saw she might have gone too far with that last comment as her friend's face took on a pink hue that could either be attributed to embarrassment or anger. Bri wasn't entirely sure which before she continued on.

"Listen, you're just scared because you never crossed over from voyeur to player. I know you, Tiff. You used to get just as turned on as I did when we'd go to the clubs and watch Doms do those exact things to other subs. Admit it. Lukus has to get your pulse racing. He's the perfect mix of strength, protectiveness, and tenderness. I've spent enough time with him, and he may try to hide it, but he has a heart. I think you're a complete and total idiot if you don't try to at least get to know him better. Maybe he won't turn out to be perfect, but just think of all of the fun you could have while you try to figure it out."

"I'm more worried about how sore my ass would be while I tried to figure it out," Tiff mumbled.

Brianna grinned playfully. "I know. Isn't it great? Like I said, you could have so much fun being naughty and then getting spanked. The best part is what comes after the spanking."

"Fine, I'll admit he got my pulse going, but he's too dangerous. I truly worry about you, Bri. You're obsessed and you're gonna keep getting hurt." Tiffany was clearly not as comfortable talking about her sexual needs with her best friend as Bri was. Her face had gone from a blushing pink to all-out red.

"What? Don't knock it until you've tried it. You actually have to come out from behind the book and live it for at least one day before you have the right to give me shit about knowing what I need. Please... trust me, Tiff."

"No offense, but you haven't been doing the best in the man category lately, so forgive me if I don't rush to take your advice. You have a husband who's angry and ready to divorce you and a blackmailing ex-boyfriend who'd love nothing more than to keep you tied up and beaten daily for the rest of what would be your very short life."

"Ladies?" Lukus's deep voice coming from the door of the bedroom startled them. The women literally flinched at the sound. They both whipped around just in time to catch his sexy smile. He was leaning against the doorjamb with his arms crossed over his broad chest.

Brianna found her voice first. "Lukus... how long have you been standing there?"

Based on his smug smile, Bri was pretty sure he'd been standing there long enough to catch the bulk of their conversation. A glance at Tiff proved she wanted to fall through the floor from embarrassment.

"Oh, not too terrible long," he answered. "But long enough to agree with you, Tiffany. I'd think twice about listening to Brianna's recommendations on men if I were you. I'm sure your sweet ass would appreciate it."

Tiffany let out a loud groan and lunged towards the head of Lukus's bed, burying her flushed face in his pillow and letting out a muffled scream. Her embarrassed and rather childish reaction caused Lukus to actually burst out laughing, which only made Tiffany scream into the pillow louder. Brianna watched with a strange mix of guilt and amusement as her best friend had a mini-meltdown reminiscent of a scene from a seventh-grade sleepover.

Bri reached out to rub her friend's back while trying to calm her down. "Come on, Tiff. You're overreacting just a tad bit, don't you think?"

Bri wasn't exactly sure of Tiffany's answer

since she was still shouting into the pillow, but it sounded suspiciously like '*fuck you, Brianna.*'

Bri turned to Lukus and tried to take her frustration out on him. "What are you doing here, Lukus?"

"Well, gee. First, I *live* here so I'm pretty sure I'm allowed to come and go as I please."

"You know what I mean. Can I go home now? I really need to talk to Markus," Bri demanded, hopeful this ordeal was over.

Lukus's expression immediately got serious. All traces of the humor he was sharing at Tiffany's expense only seconds before were gone.

"Be very careful, sweetheart. This is my only warning to watch your tone with me. While I may have been more lenient than normal with you because you're not a trained sub, don't make the mistake of thinking that gives you carte blanche to act like a brat. The next time you talk to me with that tone, I'll have you over my knee so fast, you won't know what hit you. And I assure you—it will *not* be a pleasant experience that ends in a climax. A punishment will never again end in an orgasm for you, at least not as long as I have anything to do with it."

Brianna surprised even herself with her immediate, gut response to Lukus's warning. "I'm so sorry, Sir. You're right. I was rude." Her heartfelt response was reflexive.

He took a few seconds before acknowledging.

"That's a good girl. We'll get you properly trained yet."

Brianna continued to push, but this time with the proper respect. "Sir, if I may ask... you said that *we'll* get you properly trained. Please, does that *we* include Markus? I know you saw him today. Is he going to let me come home tonight?"

Lukus's face was a mask. Brianna couldn't interpret his expression. She knew she was pushing her luck by staring directly into his eyes instead of submissively lowering her gaze, but she just couldn't look away. She needed the answers he was withholding from her.

Lukus paused, choosing his words carefully. "He's really hurting right now. I honestly don't know if he's ever going to forgive you, Brianna. He upended his entire life to be with you, and you basically said '*fuck you*' in return by being with Jake again. With time, who knows? Maybe he'll be able to believe you won't do it again."

Bri fought the tears threatening. "Did you tell him I'd *never* do it again? Didn't you tell him about why I did it? About that submissive part of me I've tried so hard to push down, but just couldn't? And about the blackmail..."

"Yeah, I told him. But I'm not entirely sure he believes me. I think you just need to give him a bit more time to think things through."

Brianna's heart was breaking. She'd been so sure Lukus would have been able to convince

Markus to forgive her. Okay, maybe not *forgive*, but to at least give her a chance to make it up to him. She'd hoped her husband would welcome a chance to embrace his dominant side again, with her, in a full-time D/s relationship. Only now did Brianna realize what a mistake it had been to allow herself to get her hopes up. She closed her eyes and tried to give herself an internal pep talk.

You just need to give him more time, Bri. You can't give up fighting yet. It's only been one day.

Her pep talk lasted approximately thirty-seconds before her fears closed in and the tears she'd held back fell.

He's going to divorce me, and I deserve it. I was so close to having it all. If only I could've been more open with him. I should have been brave enough to tell him what I was feeling... what I needed. Now he hates me.

Brianna felt rather than saw Lukus taking a seat next to her on the bed. She was grateful for his shoulder to cry on as he pulled her into his lap to comfort her, much like he'd done after her bath. She held onto him tightly as he let her cry it out before finally pulling back far enough to see her face. When she opened her eyes, she saw Lukus's sympathetic expression.

"Markus still loves you, sweetheart. I know he does. He was so worried about how you were doing, but he just isn't ready to forgive you—yet. He asked me to keep up with the punishment regime I had planned for you. He wants me to call him tomorrow to check in and I hope he'll think about everything I talked about with him today. Let's just get through your next round of punishments tonight and then we'll see what tomorrow brings." He wiped away the tears from her cheeks.

"My next punishment? Please, Lukus. What's the plan here? Is this one big, long, indefinite punishment session like Jake's cabin?"

Tiffany jumped into the conversation. "Oh, for crying out loud, Brianna! Don't you dare compare this to Jake taking you to that damn cabin. I was there when he brought you home beaten to within an inch of your life. You were bruised and bleeding for Christ's sake! I hardly think this is the same considering you're sitting here on a soft bed while Lukus holds you and comforts you. Not to mention, you actually did something wrong this time! Jake beat you nonstop for days because you forgot to pick up his fucking dry-cleaning!"

Brianna was shocked by her friend's impassioned outburst.

Lukus smiled as he answered her. "Well said, Tiffany, right up to the part where you started talking like a truck driver. I prefer my subs reserve that kind of language for when they're in the throes of passion. As long as you're my *guest*, I'd like you to follow those rules."

The look on Tiffany's face was priceless.

Brianna had seen it before and feared her friend might self-combust.

"Well, Lukus, since the last time I checked, I wasn't part of your goddamn stable of subs, I think I can use any fucking words I choose, particularly since every other word out of *your* mouth seems to be a cuss word."

Brianna watched as Tiffany defiantly took on Lukus. This might get interesting.

"You're so right. You're not one of my subs but given that I've informed you that as my guest you're expected to follow my rules, consider this your final warning. I suggest you stop acting like a brat and behave."

"Or what?"

"That's one."

"Oh, so now you're gonna count like I'm a three-year-old?"

"That's two. Keep it up."

Tiff was at least smart enough to keep her mouth shut while she contemplated her situation. Bri had a front row seat as they were locked in a battle of wills. Lukus was unflappable, but Tiffany was weighing whether to continue to assert herself or cave. The tension in the room had built to such a fever pitch that Brianna was actually relieved when Master Derek appeared in the doorway to the bedroom.

"So, what did I miss? Looks like you have your hands full here, Master Lukus."

Derek's arrival gave Tiffany a lucky reprieve as Lukus diverted his attention to her friend.

"Let's go, Brianna. Rachel is waiting downstairs. It's time for the punishment you earned this afternoon. Tiffany, I want you to stay put. I'll be back to deal with you later."

Brianna's mouth went dry with fear at the thought of being caned by Lukus. Still, an unwelcome excitement sparked inside her, despite the fear the cane incited. It had been one of Jake's favorite implements, and that alone had her trembling.

Seeing her sudden fear, Lukus tried to reassure her. "Don't worry sweetheart. After what you've gone through since last night, this should be a piece of cake for you. The only difference this time is there will be no hitting sub-space." Lukus paused, sensing a change in her. "What is it?"

When her trembling got worse, Lukus pulled her to stand in front of him. She pulled the sheet along with her. He was waiting for an answer. She knew it.

"Please be careful with the cane, Lukus. It was Jake's favorite form of torture that weekend in the cabin. It's just... my last caning ended with me sporting several dozen open cuts."

Anger and protectiveness warred in his green eyes. "Sweetheart, this is a promise. While you certainly will not enjoy this punishment, you'll *never* receive anything even close to open wounds at my hands. Do you hear me?"

"Yes," Bri whimpered.

"Do you believe me?"

Bri took a few seconds longer this time, but when she answered *Yes,* she meant it. She instinctively trusted Lukus.

Feeling better, Bri turned to hug Tiffany, trying to keep the sheet wrapped around her. "I'm so sorry to have dragged you into this whole mess, Tiff. I'm selfishly happy, though. I don't know what I'd do without you here helping me through this."

As Bri stood to follow Lukus, he changed his directions. "Master Derek, take Brianna down and get her situated. I'd like a word with Tiffany... alone. I'll be right behind you."

"You got it, boss. Come along, little girl." Bri gave Tiff and Lukus one last glance before she left ahead of Master Derek. She sure hoped Tiff behaved herself and didn't find out what happened at the count of three.

Tiffany

Tiffany watched with trepidation as her best friend left with the huge hulk of a man. Even knowing Bri was going to be caned a dozen times, Tiff wasn't entirely sure she wouldn't prefer to trade places with her friend at this moment. The look Lukus was giving her seemed more ominous than the cane.

Just keep your damn mouth shut, Tiffany. Stop trying to poke the bear.

Once alone, Lukus took a seat, facing Tiff on the bed. "I see you've thought better of pushing me to three." The jerk smirked while acknowledging her small achievement.

His eyes were boring into her, testing her ability to remain quiet. She had to fight down the urge to tell him to screw off because she instinctually knew he wasn't making an idle threat. She might not know exactly *what* would happen if he got to three, but she was pretty sure she wouldn't like it.

Or would she? She hated to admit it, even to herself, but Bri had been right. While she might have only experienced parts of the BDSM lifestyle vicariously through books and Bri, that didn't mean she wasn't curious. Scratch that—she was more than curious. There had been a time when she'd wanted to explore her submissive tendencies every bit as much as her best friend. Only watching the hell that Bri had gone through at the hands of Jake had helped push her desire down. Since then, the closest she'd ever gotten to reality was a lame spanking at the hands of Jason. He had only done it to please her, but the spanking was so anti-climactic that she'd written the whole thing off as a complete failure.

So why did she find herself biting her tongue to keep from pushing him to three? It would have been so easy. Luckily, Lukus spoke before she could open her mouth again.

"I see it in your eyes, Tiffany. You're fighting it. You want me to get to three, don't you?" Her breath hitched as Lukus watched her drowning in the conflicting emotions that had to be parading across her face before continuing. "While I do realize you're neither my sub nor a club member, you are a guest in my home. I therefore expect you to behave yourself accordingly. There are consequences, even for houseguests, for broken rules. Understood?"

What she was tempted to say was, '*screw you, you big bully.*' What came out was, "Yes, Sir." While self-loathing invaded for caving in, she quickly became grateful for choosing the submissive route when she was rewarded with one of the sexiest smiles she'd ever seen. A warm glow of pleasure washed over her at Lukus's obvious approval of her submission. The warmth flowed through her, settling squarely at the apex of her pressed-together thighs. The submissive sensation was new, but didn't feel wrong.

Their eyes locked as Lukus reached out to brush a strand of hair away from her face. Before her scrambled brain could think of something clever to say, he was on his feet, stalking to the door.

Only when he was almost gone did Tiff know what she wanted to say.

"Lukus?" She called out.

Already half out the door, he turned back to give her his attention. He waited patiently for her to spit it out. "Lukus. If you hurt her... I mean *really* hurt her... I'll never forgive you."

He slowly walked back to Tiffany who was still sitting on her knees near the edge of his messed-up bed. His face was a mask. She couldn't tell if he was angry or not, but it didn't matter. She had needed to warn him. Still, the intensity of his gaze drove her to look down at her hands, wringing in her lap.

Tiff startled when he reached out to cup her cheek, pulling her face up, until she again met his gaze. The previously absent tenderness in his eyes was a welcome comfort.

"Baby. If I really hurt her... *I'd* never forgive myself."

Her sharp intake of breath was her only response as Lukus dropped his hand and quickly strode out of the room, leaving Tiffany with a racing heart and a completely overwhelmed mind.

I'm in so much trouble here. The man is like a freaking irresistible magnet. Be careful, Tiff!

CHAPTER EIGHT

BRIANNA

By the time Brianna and Derek reached the dungeon, Brianna had worked herself into a near panic attack. With each step she took, the unwanted memories of her last caning at the hands of Jake returned. While the open wounds had healed with time, the internal scarring was harder to treat. As they passed through the backstage area, Bri slowed, subconsciously trying to delay the inevitable. Eventually she came to a dead stop in the wide doorway leading to the stage, causing Derek to walk into her back.

"All right, naughty girl. Keep it moving. You earned this punishment so there'll be no stalling."

When she remained frozen, Derek, unaware of her internal struggle, grasped her hips and propelled her forward.

At least the club was still dark. This punishment was going to be hard enough to get through without having a hoard of witnesses watching, getting turned on by her tears and screams.

Rachel was already there. Like the good little submissive she was, she was already naked and properly positioned, bent over the padded spanking bench with her arms and legs spread to the corners of the device, leaving her ass and the back of her legs completely vulnerable to her punishers. Rachel looked up at the sound of them approaching. Her glance immediately sought out her husband's as tears flooded her beautiful eyes, quickly spilling over and down her cheeks.

Derek grabbed Brianna's upper arm, pulling her to a stop. "Wait here. I need to speak with my wife privately."

Bri didn't miss the disappointment in his voice and when she sneaked a quick peek up at his face, she found a strange mix of anger and concern. She certainly didn't know Derek well, but it was easy to see he was not happy his sub had contributed to this day's craziness.

Brianna tried to look away to give them some degree of privacy, but since she was only about six feet from where Rachel was awaiting her doom, there was not much privacy to be had. She turned to the side, taking her eyes off them completely, but short of putting her hands over her ears, she couldn't help but hear their exchange.

Derek's voice was stiff and controlled as he addressed his wife. "Stand up, little girl."

Bri could hear Rachel lifting off the spanking bench and she could only guess she was avoiding her husband's gaze because his next instructions were impatient.

"Look at me right now, Rachel Lynn."

"I'm so sorry, Daddy. I really am." Bri detected the quaver in her voice.

"I just bet you are now that you were caught red-handed. Were my instructions unclear?"

Brianna could tell Derek was trying to keep their conversation private because he was speaking more softly than she had thought possible for him. Still, they were close enough that she could hear every word.

"No, Sir."

"So, you just blatantly defied me because you were in the mood to have your ass lit up?"

Bri could hear Rachel crying. "No, Sir. I really didn't plan to disobey. I accidentally dropped a coffee mug in the kitchen, and it woke her up. She was calling out for Master Lukus. I know I should've just ignored her calling, but I thought maybe something was wrong, so I was peeking in, just to check on her, and she saw me."

"Enough. You know I don't put up with excuses. The instructions were clear. You defied them. I told you there were very good reasons Lukus didn't want you talking to her."

"I know, Sir, but I promise. I didn't say anything about Master Markus other than what she already knew."

"And just what exactly was that?"

"She already knew that Master Markus came here with Georgie." Brianna could hear the panic in Rachel's voice.

"Rachel Lynn Parker, you aren't going to sit on that beautiful little ass of yours for a week if I find out you told her anything about Master Markus and Georgie—and you know exactly what I mean."

Their voices were getting even softer and Brianna had to really strain now to hear the next part of the conversation, but considering they were talking about *her* husband, she didn't feel the least bit guilty.

"I swear to you, Daddy. I didn't tell her anything about what happened the last night Master Markus was here with his ex-wife."

"You'd better not. That's not our secret to tell. Markus is gonna have to come clean on that one on his own. You just keep your pretty little nose out of it, do you hear me young lady?"

"Yes, Sir. I promise."

Oh, my God! What secret are they talking about? It has to be something serious to have Derek that concerned about it coming out.

Bri didn't have nearly long enough to evaluate the possibilities before she was surprised by the next question Derek directed to his wife. "How are you feeling? Are you okay or do we need to do this later?" That seemed like a strangely gentle question for the hard-ass Dom to ask his naughty sub as she was about to be punished.

"No, Sir. I'm just getting a bit tired, but I'm feeling okay today."

"Well, remember what we discussed, little girl. I want you to safeword immediately if you want us to stop. There'll be no getting out of your punishment completely, but we can break it up into several sessions if we need to. Understand?"

"Yes, Sir. Thank you, Sir."

A few long seconds ticked by before Brianna picked up the erotic sound of the couple passionately kissing behind her. She took a chance and glanced over her shoulder to catch a glimpse of Derek and Rachel's embrace. All thoughts of fear temporarily evaporated to be replaced by an immense yearning for her own husband as she watched Derek tightly holding Rachel against his muscular body. He was so large compared to her petite frame and had one hand tightly grasping Rachel's ass as she raised her leg to wrap it around his waist. His other hand had her long hair pulled back so hard that her creamy neck was exposed to her Dom. He sucked and kissed the vulnerable spot where her shoulder met her neck as Rachel humped against his body. Both were moaning with pleasure.

The amorous sounds were intoxicating.

Brianna tried not to listen, not to think about how lucky her new friend was right now. Brianna had just brought her fingers up to stroke her own wet pussy when Lukus decided to join them on stage.

"Brianna Lambert, stop touching yourself this very minute or I'll be adding strokes."

Brianna realized her face must have been bright red with embarrassment at being caught masturbating. She wished the ground would open up and swallow her whole rather than have to look at Lukus.

She wondered if anyone could blame her given the sexual tension that had been ramping up all day.

She spent the day buck naked while *almost* enjoying the tight ropes binding her breasts, a constant reminder of her impending punishment. And as if all of that wasn't bad enough, Lukus had belted her to near orgasm before leaving her to stew in her own juices, literally.

What does he expect? I dare him to live through that and not be as horny as hell.

Luckily, she was able to avoid eye contact with Lukus. He luckily ignored her as he walked straight to Derek and Rachel, who reluctantly tore themselves apart after Lukus cleared his throat. Brianna was completely stunned when Lukus reached out to pull Rachel into a big bear hug.

"Derek told me the great news. I'm so happy for you, Rachel."

"Thank you, Master Lukus." She smiled, hugging him back.

Pulling out of the hug to look down into her eyes, Lukus continued, "How are you feeling?"

Rachel's smile took on a glow. "I'm fine, Sir. Really, I am, but thank you for asking."

"Don't think for one minute your news is gonna get you out of a punishment, but..." Lukus took a short break to look up at Derek before continuing on. "I called James before coming down. I wanted to consult with him on the proper way to handle Rachel's punishments now. We'll be making some modifications as a result of his recommendations on how he handled punishments with Mary... but..." Lukus turned his attention back to Rachel as he continued on with his scolding. "You're in big trouble, young lady. Still, no matter what, you have to promise me you'll safeword if you need us to stop. Do you understand?"

"Yes, Sir. Master Derek just explained the same thing."

Brianna was confused with the exchange and began feeling a bit persecuted. "Why does she get to safeword out of her punishment, but if I do, I have to get divorced?"

Lukus shot her an annoyed look. "Not that we were talking to you, Miss Nosey, but I just found out Rachel is expecting a baby."

Wow, I sure didn't see that coming.

For a moment, Brianna forgot where she was as

she rushed forward to hug Rachel. "Oh, what great news! Congratulations, Rachel." Pulling out of the hug, the naked women looked each other in the eye. "How far along are you?"

"Only about three months." Rachel's voice was full of a shy excitement.

"Well, that's wonderful news. I'm so happy for you." She turned to Derek. "Congratulations to you too, Derek. You look so happy."

After her informal comment, she quickly added a fast "Sir" hoping it would suffice to appease him in case he was offended, but he wasn't. It was easy to see he was thrilled at his wife's condition, if not a tad bit uneasy at the attention it was bringing him.

"Thanks, Brianna. I'm scared shitless I'm going to screw the poor kid up, but with any luck, I'll get the hang of the parenting thing before I actually do any lasting harm."

Brianna couldn't stop grinning at his contagious excitement. "I'm sure you'll do great, Sir."

Lukus dragged their attention back to the task at hand, quickly dousing the joy Bri and Rachel had been feeling by reminding the women they were both in trouble. She hadn't seen him leave, but when Bri looked over, Lukus was hauling in a second spanking bench from backstage. He dragged it directly opposite the already placed bench. He moved them so close, they were almost touching.

"Okay, sweetheart. Get your soon-to-be-red ass over here."

Brianna's pulse notched up in anticipation of what was to come.

When she was slow to move towards him, he reminded her to hurry. "I'd stop stalling if I were you or we'll start adding strokes for tardiness."

Brianna crossed the few feet separating them quickly. As soon as she was within reach, Lukus grabbed her, roughly lining her up with the end of the long bench. He took a minute to adjust the leather padded top so the end where her head was at a forty-five-degree angle. Bri saw Derek doing the same on Rachel's bench.

As the tops of the benches were facing each other, Brianna quickly realized the men would be punishing both women at the same time while they were forced to watch the effects of the other's punishment. Her eyes sought out Rachel's, finding a resigned look on the expectant mother's face as she mentally prepared for her caning.

When he had the bench set up, Lukus reached back and took Brianna's hand to pull her forward. She tried hard not to let him see her trembling. She'd love to blame her shivers on the club's chill, but she couldn't. It was actually a comfortably warm temperature and she assumed that wasn't an accident. Considering so many submissives, both men and women, came to the club with little-to-no clothes on, Brianna was sure Lukus kept the temperature comfortable for them.

As Brianna approached the punishment bench, Lukus guided her to straddle the now angled top and kneel on the padded leg rests. She leaned forward, placing her weight on the cool leather, as she reached for the handgrips on either side of the bench near her head.

Brianna was uneasy when Lukus began strapping her into place, tightly securing both her ankles and wrists to the bench. The position of her legs had her splayed wide, vulnerable. She was almost completely immobile when Lukus's chest unexpectedly brushed her back as he reached below her to grasp the wide leather waist restraint. He cinched it tightly, securing her waist to the bench and ensuring she wouldn't be able to yank her ass away from the upcoming blows, no matter how much she may want to.

Brianna's anxiety escalated as she looked up and realized she was only about two feet away from Rachel's face. Rachel's expression was not much better as her husband secured her to her own bench in the exact same manner. It didn't bode well that such an experienced submissive was afraid of her upcoming discipline.

Brianna was embarrassed to have Rachel there to witness her lose control, which she was surely going to do since Lukus had promised to keep her from escaping to her happy place and climaxing.

Yet, a part of her was comforted that she wouldn't be going through this punishment alone. She felt a budding sisterhood with Rachel nearby.

An unwelcome memory of Jake invaded as she heard Lukus standing behind her, swishing a medium-weight cane through the open air, testing the feel of the punishment device. Just the swishing was a frightening trigger, bringing back buried feelings.

Brianna closed her eyes, trying to remain calm as she remembered how brutal his punishments had been. A deep anger towards Jake burned inside of her. His repeated abuse had conditioned her body to cope in the only way it knew how when faced with the overwhelming dose of pain; unknowingly, he'd tapped into the ability to drive her to her happy place, where intense orgasms would run together, creating a sensation that was akin to a drug-induced high.

Her brain had always known how dangerous Jake was, but over time, she found she could only push down her desire for that intense pleasure for so long before she needed another *hit*. She felt a renewed shame at allowing the need for those powerful orgasms to outweigh the danger of going anywhere with Jake ever again.

No wonder Markus will never forgive me. I'm not sure I'll ever forgive myself.

"Brianna, are you okay?" It was Rachel asking, having a front row seat to the look of rising fear on her face.

"I've just had a really bad history with a cane is all. It's freaking me out."

She immediately felt Lukus's warm caress on the small of her back. "Brianna, I told you I'd be careful. You told me you trust me. Was that a lie?" His voice was surprisingly gentle.

Tears were streaming down her face as she answered. "I didn't lie, Sir, but that doesn't stop me from being afraid. I just can't help but remember."

"Well, today is the day you're going to forget about Jake. Do you hear me? Focus on the here and now." He turned and addressed Derek. "You want to tag team this one?"

Derek was quick to reply. "I was hoping that's what you were thinking when you brought in the second bench. Since Rachel has more to go, I'll start. I think we'd better give them a warm-up first, don't you?"

Lukus's answer came in the form of a hard slap to Brianna's ass with his open palm. Derek wasted no time in getting started with Rachel's spanking as well.

At first, Brianna just thought they were trying to prolong the women's punishment, but then she remembered reading on a domestic discipline website that the head of the household should always give a warm-up spanking when they plan on using harsher implements, since it reduces the chance of bruising. Bri was grateful that, once again, Lukus was proving to be a conscientious Dom by looking out for her.

Bri closed her eyes, trying to focus on the submissive feelings coursing through her. The rather light and almost sensuous spanking was just what she needed to help her mentally prepare for what was coming next. It helped that Lukus stopped every so often to caress her ass, testing the heat level of her exposed skin.

After just a couple of minutes of warm up, Lukus and Derek stopped at the same time as if they'd choreographed it. Hell, for all Bri knew, maybe they had.

Lukus began his stern lecture to both wayward ladies. "Rachel, why are you being punished today?"

"Because I disobeyed direct orders from Master Derek. I not only let Brianna see me, but I talked with her and I also untied her from the bed. I'm so very sorry, Sir."

"That's correct. I'm sure you are sorry and if you aren't yet, you will be very soon. Brianna, why are you being punished today?"

"Because I coaxed Rachel into coming into the bedroom and talking to me and then untying me, even though I knew you'd never want her to."

"That's correct. I didn't hear your apology. Do you want additional strokes?"

"Oh my God, no. I'm so sorry." At the last second, she remembered to throw in the "Sir."

"Better. Master Derek, let's get started. James suggests changing Rachel's punishment to a strapping or belting. Canes are off limits until after the baby comes. We also need to take frequent breaks to allow her to adjust to the pain levels. He asked that you phone him next week to sync up on his punishment advice, especially for the third trimester."

She expected to see the relief on Rachel's face, but wasn't expecting the happiness exuding from Derek with the change in plans. Only now did Bri see how much the fearless Dom had been dreading punishing his pregnant wife. Lukas waited for Derek to trade in his cane for a wide leather strap. It looked well-worn and Bri didn't even hazard a guess how many asses that leather had kissed.

Without further delay or practice taps, Derek got started with a rather hard first whack of the strap to his wife's bare ass. Brianna couldn't believe Rachel remained silent, in spite of the pained look that crossed her beautiful face. She barely had time to register the pain of the first strike when Derek delivered number two and then a quick number three. Rachel's expression changed as the pain settled in. The tears were already flowing unchecked down her face, but Bri suspected a good portion of those tears were caused from the guilt she felt at letting her Dom down by disobeying orders.

Derek continued to deliver the corporal

punishment to his wife's immobile ass. By the time he got to the tenth stroke, Rachel's tears were flowing harder and she was whimpering with a strange mix of pain and pleasure.

Brianna was absolutely ashamed that the sight and sounds of Rachel's punishment were causing her own pussy to physically throb. By the time Derek had delivered stroke number twelve with the leather, Bri's breathing was ragged, as if she were the one on the receiving end of his corrective discipline. She felt guilty getting turned on by witnessing someone else's pain.

She didn't have long to feel the crush of guilt because she had her own agony to manage once Lukus got started. She heard the swish of the upcoming stroke before she felt it. The short warning, unfortunately, gave her enough time to clench her ass. There was a delay of about one second where Bri's brain had just enough time to think, '*Well that wasn't so bad,*' before the heat spread across her ass like a lick of fire. She barely finished that thought before the second stroke fell just below the first. Brianna vaguely registered that Lukus really was a pro, grateful he had avoided hitting the same place twice.

It was on the third stroke that Brianna let out an involuntary cry, yanking as hard as she could against the leather restraints in a futile attempt to free herself from their restrictive hold. Lukus payed her cry no mind and quickly delivered number four with a very loud *thwack* that echoed through the empty chamber.

Both women were one-third through the punishment.

True to his word, Lukus didn't help her by rubbing away the pain, but as he turned the scene over to Derek to deliver the next set to Rachel, he stepped close to Brianna to comfort her by lightly rubbing the small of her back. His touch was strangely soothing considering he was touching her with the exact same hand that was causing her pain in the first place. She was grateful for the short reprieve to try to get her emotions in check, yet it was difficult to truly calm down as Rachel cried through her continued strapping.

"Oh please, Daddy. I'm so sorry. Please... no more." The tone of her plea was heartbreaking.

Rachel couldn't see Derek's face, but Brianna could. Derek looked as if he were in pain, just like his wife. While she'd noticed him almost relishing punishing other subs on stage the night before, Bri could see he was enjoying this punishment about as much as his wayward sub. Still, he steeled his jaw and pulled back his muscular arm to deliver another loud strapping to his wife's ass. The next four strokes came at about ten-second intervals with Rachel crying hard by the time he got to his next stopping point at twenty-four lashes. When Rachel struggled against her binds, Brianna wished her hands were free so she could reach across and comfort the young submissive. She was relieved to see Derek caressing his wife's back lightly just as Lukus had done, helping Rachel get her tears under control.

It was almost like the men made a pact ahead of time not to talk during the punishment because within one minute of Derek finishing, Lukus silently removed his caressing hand to resume Brianna's caning. This time, the first strike connected perfectly with Brianna's tender sit spot where her ass and thighs met. The scream that erupted from her was primal.

It was in the aftermath of that stroke she felt a welcome warmth growing, igniting her pussy to the same heat level as her punished ass. She recognized the signs that she was on her way to sub-space around the same time Lukus issued a warning. "I told you, and I expect you to remember, you will never come again during a punishment. I'd be very careful. Hold it back, Brianna."

How the hell could he know so fast?

Through her pain Brianna gritted out, "I can't. It hurts so much, Lukus. Please... stop..."

"Sorry sweetheart, but it's supposed to hurt. That's why it's called a punishment. If this were a sensual or erotic caning, you'd be allowed to come as many times as you want." Lukus delivered the next stroke as Brianna tried to wrap her head around the fact that someone...*anyone*... might actually try to combine the words "sensual" and "caning" into one sentence. It seemed ridiculous to her as tears finally fell down her cheeks through the eighth and hardest stroke yet, bringing her to her two-thirds point.

Lukus leaned down to quietly ask against her ear, "Are you doing okay, sweetheart, or would you like a short break before we finish?"

Bri couldn't keep the surprise out of her answer. "You're actually asking me? I have a choice?"

Lukus's voice was stronger when he replied. "We will finish. Of that you have no choice. But I'm not an ogre, Brianna. The purpose of a punishment is for a sub to learn her lesson. That doesn't mean I need to terrorize you to get my point across."

Brianna's breath caught.

Why the hell couldn't I have met Lukus instead of Jake at that club all those years ago? He's the Dom I'd been dreaming of. I got stuck with the devil instead.

"Let's just get it over with. I really hate how you're stopping me from going to my happy place."

Lukus's light caress on her cheek was as odd as his soft chuckle. "There is no happy place in a punishment. That only comes once your punishment is over."

Their conversation was cut short by the sound of the strap connecting solidly with Rachel's ass. Bri's eyes connected with her fellow sister-in-arms in time to see the flood of emotions bombarding Rachel. The surprise, the burn on her ass, and after a few long seconds, the resignation of her situation. The tears were falling down her cheeks and Brianna was just thinking about how much she wanted to reach out and comfort her new friend when her own ass felt the agony of her own next cane strike at the hands of Lukus. This strike felt much harder than the previous eight and the involuntary scream left her before she could stop herself. Now she wished she could wipe away her own tears.

The men continued alternating back and forth with their punishment. While in the beginning Brianna could tell Lukus was trying to keep the welts from hitting one on top of the next, her ass and upper thighs were now so covered with pain that she could no longer distinguish where one painful stripe ended and the next began.

When she could no longer take it, Bri started rambling. "No... please, Sir... I'm begging you... no more." When it was clear he wasn't stopping, her ranting moved to apologies—apologies she truly meant. "I'm so sorry. Please, Sir, it hurts too much. I promise to behave."

It hit Bri at some point that as bad as she had it right now, Rachel had had it much worse. Even though she was being strapped and not caned, this could have been more pain than a pregnant woman should withstand and Bri suddenly understood the extra care and concern both Doms had shown Rachel before the punishment had even begun. In spite of the agony Lukus was causing her right now, she felt a wave of affection over his concern for Rachel.

Close to done, she focused on just getting through the final few strokes. When Lukus finally announced she'd completed her punishment, there was a tiny part of her that was actually sorry because the last few strokes had heated her pussy.

Only when she felt Lukus caressing her now slick slit did she understand he'd done it on purpose. He barely brushed her clit with the pad of his finger and an involuntary shudder passed through her as he chuckled, pulling his hand away.

"Damn you, Lukus. You did that on purpose."

The unexpected cane strike took her breath away. "Oweeee! I thought I was done!"

Lukus leaned close and grabbed her chin to turn her wet face towards him. She had no choice but to look him in the eye. "Next lesson, sweetheart. At least when you're being punished, I'm not Lukus. I am Sir or Master. And when your Master spends his valuable time correcting your misbehavior, you'll thank him. Is that clear?"

Brianna was shocked at how easily her words tumbled from her mouth. It was as if she'd been waiting for his direction. "I'm so sorry, Sir. Thank you for punishing me, Sir."

Brianna was rewarded with a signature Lukus

smile that lit up his green eyes. In spite of his earlier rant about Doms rubbing their subs' pain away, Bri welcomed his tender touch lightly massaging her ass and thighs. She could tell he was inspecting his handy work to make sure he hadn't done any lasting damage. A warm rush flowed through her at the mere possibility her husband might one day punish her like this. In spite of the lingering discomfort, she felt a fulfillment she'd been searching for washing over her. This dangerous intimacy—the connection she felt to Lukus right now—is what she'd been dreaming of. It was a level of intimacy she longed to experience with Markus.

Poor Rachel's punishment was continuing. Only now did Bri sneak another peek at Derek and she was still confused at the pain she saw on his face. She'd always assumed that Doms like Lukus and Derek were sadists, men who got their kicks by actually hurting their subs. She knew she had gotten that idea because that was exactly what drove Jake. But she was learning they could be gentle and caring as well.

These men were so different, and she couldn't help but wonder what kind of Dom Markus had been. Surely, he had to have been more like Lukus and Derek. If he had been a true sadist, she doubted he could've turned his back on the lifestyle.

Derek finally reached the end and called out a loud "thirty-six," dropping the leather strap as if it was burning him. He rushed to his wife's side, stroking her back lightly to comfort her, leaning in to place gentle kisses on the back of her head. It took her several long seconds to calm enough to speak and her first words were an apology. "I'm so sorry for disobeying you, Daddy. I promise I'll do better next time. Thank you for punishing me, Master."

Bri didn't miss the slight catch in Derek's voice as he answered. "I know, little one. Daddy still loves his little girl very much. You took your punishment like a very good submissive."

Lukus's continued light caresses to Brianna's lower back had helped her calm down. "Very good. You girls need to stay here and spend the next ten minutes quietly thinking about why you were punished. Derek is going to keep an eye on you and will release you when your reflection time is up. I'm gonna go upstairs and find some food for all of us since I'm guessing everyone is as hungry as I am. We need to eat before it's time to get ready for tonight's show."

Lukus strode out before Brianna could question him. Her heart was racing, remembering this punishment had nothing to do with Markus. Bri remembered Lukus's earlier comments about continuing on with her planned punishment regime tonight. She felt a mixture of excitement and dread of what would happen to her on stage tonight at the hands of her husband's best friend.

The mere thought of any additional punishment to her burning ass was frightening, especially knowing there would be an audience the next time.

In her quiet reflection time, a welcome calm washed over Bri when she realized she didn't need to worry about it. Lukus would do what he wanted to do to her body, and she would submit. She pondered the differences between Jake and Lukus. There were many, but there was one key difference that was more important than all of the other differences combined. It was *trust*. Bri *trusted* Lukus to know what she needed. She *trusted* him to understand her limits, *trusted* him to never truly hurt her. Yes, trust was what made all the difference in the world.

Please, God, give me a chance to see if I can trust Markus as a Dom the same way I trust his best friend.

CHAPTER NINE

LUKUS

Lukus was quite pleased with himself as he headed up to his loft. He was amazed by the speed at which Brianna was learning to bend to the rules of the D/s lifestyle. She was so different from so many of the subs that passed through The Punishment Pit each night. She was doing a fine job of walking the tightrope of staying true to her core self while exploring her natural submissive side. Markus was one lucky bastard. He was gonna have so much fun training her properly.

That sassy little mouth of hers is gonna get her into some interesting punishments to be sure.

She wasn't the only one with a sassy mouth. It wasn't lost on Lukus that for about the last half of Brianna's punishment, it had actually been her best friend's curvy body he'd been imagining strapped down to the spanking bench. A wave of desire to see Tiffany spread wide for him—vulnerable, submissive, and whimpering just like Brianna—washed over him. His cock was already as hard as steel and the memory of Tiffany's earlier untrained submission made his next planned stop—his master bathroom to jack off.

There's no way I'm going to make it through tonight's festivities without embarrassing myself if I don't give myself some relief. How pathetic that I need to masturbate twice in one day? It's gotta be a new fucking record for me.

He knew he needed to push all thoughts of Tiffany down for now. He'd have to wait to think about her tomorrow, or next week. Maybe later he could explore whether Tiffany might hold the key to what had been eluding him. But not tonight. Until this Markus crap was wrapped up, he couldn't lose focus. He didn't have the luxury of the time it would take to properly contemplate the complexities she might bring to his life right now.

He hadn't even finished his thought when he rounded the corner of his great room to look up and find Tiffany standing at the stove in his gourmet kitchen, looking *exactly* like she belonged there. The unexpected scene nearly knocked him on his ass. She'd gathered her long, gently curly blonde hair into a messy and very sexy up-do with wisps of tendrils spilling down to frame her face. Her close-fitting wrap-around dress was showcasing her curvy body, making him want to bend her over the kitchen counter and slam his cock into her again and again until they were both spent.

Probably not the best way to get on her good side, sport, considering you've only known her for a few hours.

Tiffany looked up as he approached. A tentative smile lit up her face. All traces of her previous flustered embarrassment appeared to have evaporated and he wasn't exactly sure how he felt about that. The person standing in front of him was no giddy teenager that had just got caught in her undies. No, she was all woman. He hated that he didn't know her well enough to detect if she was intentionally flaunting her newfound confidence as a challenge, or if he was just witnessing her natural demeanor. Either way, it was sexy as hell and had the unwanted effect of making *him* feel like a giddy teenager.

Get a grip, Mitchell. Doms don't normally get knocked on their ass by fully clothed sub wanna-be's simply making them dinner. But God damn, I want this woman. Markus... focus on Markus.

"Oh good, you're back. I hope you don't mind, but I was starving, and Brianna told me before she left with you that she was hungry, too. I was bored while you were gone and decided to get up and forage for something. I found some hamburger in the freezer and the fixings to make spaghetti and a salad. I figured everyone would want to eat something soon. Hope you like pasta."

Her assertive confidence was confusing to Lukus. While he wanted to lash out at her for daring to make herself at home in his kitchen without prior permission or orders from him, he quickly pushed the urge down. He recognized a feeling of unexpected contentment as he watched her maneuvering around his loft as if she's lived here for years. He didn't even have time to comment before she continued on.

"I have to tell you. You have a dream kitchen, Lukus. I've always loved to cook, but recently fell into a rut where it just wasn't as much fun, especially just cooking for myself. I walked into this space and it just screamed at me to cook something. Do you like to cook, too?"

Such a simple question, but Lukus found himself too tongue-tied to answer. He stood there, silently watching her, as he tried to make sense of the rush of emotions he felt just having her there.

Tiffany chuckled. "I didn't think it was that hard of a question. Want me to make it multiple choice for you?" She delivered the taunt with just the right amount of charm and sass to pull it off.

Finally finding his voice, he answered. "I don't think that'll be necessary, Miss Smarty-Pants. I actually do like to cook. Can't say I'm exactly professional chef material, but I think I can hold my own."

"I thought so. You have a nicely stocked pantry. I checked a few expiration dates and everything looks fresh, so I assumed you must do some amount of cooking at home. I know women who'd kill for this kitchen."

Lukus decided to dish it back. "Hopefully you aren't one of them. I'm not armed at the moment."

"Cute." And then, before his very eyes, he saw Tiff's entire demeanor change over to fear. "Wait. Where's Brianna? Is she okay?"

Lukus was used to seeing fear in a submissive's eyes. It was a key ingredient of the attraction to the D/s lifestyle for him—that feeling of power he commanded when he walked into a room. He'd worked hard to learn how to push subs just over the line into the fear zone that got their hearts racing while stopping short of actually overwhelming them with a level of fear where it was no longer fun. He was very good at what he did. So why did the fear in this woman's eyes make him uncomfortable?

"Brianna is fine, Tiffany. I promised you she would be."

The relief on her face was palpable. "Sorry. I didn't mean... I'm just so used to Jake hurting her... I mean..."

Lukus could feel the control exchange between them as he watched her get increasingly flustered, her assertiveness eroding. He was stunned that he genuinely wanted to stop her from free-falling back into her more submissive mode, at least for now.

He'd truly been enjoying the witty banter with the confident Tiffany.

"Tiff, don't sweat it. I've learned enough about Jake in the last twenty-four hours to know he's a complete prick who belongs in jail. Please, don't judge every Dom—strike that—don't judge *me* with the same standard you judge him with. I know you don't know shit about me, but know this: I take my responsibility as a Dom very seriously. I would never terrorize a sub like Jake does. It makes me sick we could even be lumped into the same category by anyone... especially by you or Brianna."

"I'm sorry. I owe you an apology, Lukus. You're right that I barely know you at all, but I've learned one thing about you already." Lukus was relieved to see a shy smile cross her lips. "Okay, maybe two things."

"And what, may I ask is that?"

"You do take your responsibility as a Dom seriously. I couldn't believe Brianna when she was telling me all of the things you've done to punish her. And yet, in spite of it all she said she still somehow trusts you. I thought she was crazy, like maybe you had brainwashed her or something. But I think I'm beginning to understand why she feels that way because... well... I sort of feel that way, too."

Lukus registered how very pleased he was with her answer. "And? You said you learned two things."

He could see the indecision about how to answer fluttering across her beautiful face. He was struck by the desire to close the few feet between them to take her in his arms and kiss her. The desire only got stronger when she teased him with a growing grin. "I learned you drive like a Nascar driver. It's a miracle we both survived the trip into the city." The playful twinkle in her eye as she teased him was intoxicating for the Dom and he was just ready to say, "Fuck it" and snatch her to him when he heard the elevator arriving and the voices of Derek, Rachel, and Brianna as they prepared to join them.

He was forced to settle for delivering a devilish grin. "Driving isn't all I do dangerously, baby. I can see you're enjoying playing in the shark tank with me." Lukus's flirting was meant to test her, to see just how far she'd go before she backed down. He was pleased when she met his hard stare without so much as a flinch.

"Oh, I'm a pretty good swimmer. I think I can hold my own in the shark tank with you, Lukus." Tiffany got the last word with her flirty answer. Her eyes were dancing with mischief as the others joined them. He could detect her pleasure at going another round with the Dom, once again, coming away with an unscathed ass.

Lukus glanced up and was happy Derek thought to put the girls in robes before coming up to the loft. Stepping away from her, Lukus took a seat at the massive island directly across from the stove where Tiffany would be resuming her food prep. He watched with interest as Tiffany went to hug Brianna. The friends had an exchange he couldn't hear.

Derek headed to the fridge. "Hey, man. You want a beer? I hope you don't mind, but I could really use a drink."

"Help yourself. I'll take one too. You guys hungry? Tiffany is making us dinner."

Lukus tried to keep his voice neutral, but he didn't miss the warning look Derek threw him over his shoulder on his way to the fridge. It looked something like, *'You'd better be keeping your fucking dick in your pants, man.'*

Rachel was the one who answered him. "I'm starving. It really smells good in here. I can't believe how much my appetite has increased already. I dread getting fat. I hope you aren't going to get grossed out when I start putting on weight, Daddy."

Derek delivered a beer to Lukus before walking to his wife and taking her into his arms. "Little girl, I can't wait. You know I'm a boob guy and you've already started growing in all the right places." He boldly caressed her tender breast with one hand while holding her in a tight embrace with his other hand. "I can't wait to feel the baby growing and moving inside you. You've been calling me Daddy for years. I can't believe soon, I really will be one."

CHAPTER TEN

TIFFANY

Tiffany couldn't take her eyes off of the newest couple to join them. She hadn't even officially met Rachel or Derek yet, but she was confused by the tenderness in the couple's exchange, particularly since Derek looked like a menacing mercenary with his muscular build, edgy tattoos, and badass attitude. Up to this point, her only impression of Rachel had been a quiet, fearful submissive.

Tiff was surprised by this new, more confident and playful side of the sub. It was especially strange considering the fact she was just returning from a punishment. A feeling something akin to relief passed through Tiff at she realized her stereotypical view of submissives might have been off base.

"Mmm." Brianna walked over to her best friend. "It smells great in here, Tiff. I'm starving. What are you making?"

"Nothing fancy," she said. "Just spaghetti and a salad. I even found a chocolate brownie mix and thought about whipping that up for dessert. I could really use a chocolate fix right about now." Lowering her voice, she leaned into Brianna and asked quietly, "How are you? Was it terrible?"

Bri couldn't hide the truth from her friend. "I won't lie. It was awful. I never realized how much I depend on being able to hit my happy place to get through punishments. Still, I feel strangely comforted that I did the crime, and then I did the time. Now it's over. That part of the lifestyle I like. And look, Derek had been so angry with Rachel, but once she's punished, it's like they can move past it and all is forgiven. I just pray Markus gives me another chance. I'd go through ten times as many canings of he'd just give me a chance to prove to him how much I love him, and how sorry I am."

Tiffany hugged her friend. "I'm sure he'll come around, like Lukus said. He's just hurting right now while it's so fresh, but with a little bit of time, he'll miss you and want to make it work."

"I hope so, Tiff. I honestly don't know what I'll do if he doesn't. I can't even imagine my life without him in it."

"Don't even try to. You can worry about that if and when you need to. Right now, just focus on getting through tonight. Did Lukus tell you what's gonna happen?"

"No, and I'm not even sure I want him to. It's

bad enough going through it, but if he tells me in advance, I'll just get worked up and worried. I'll tell you, though; I *hate* the idea of him punishing me in front of everyone at the club again. The punishment part is bad enough but being on stage and having people witnessing my loss of control during the punishment is ten times worse."

An involuntary shudder ran through Tiffany at her friend's words. "I can't even imagine it. It reminds me of how Beauty was always on display at the palace. I so wanted to hate that damn book as I read it, but I can't deny I had to masturbate at least once a chapter. Damn, I think I creamed my panties just thinking about it."

The girls shared a naughty giggle at Tiffany's predicament. "Well, let's pray he doesn't have you sitting in the audience watching me tonight. That would just be over-the-top weird."

"No shit. I'd end up getting into trouble myself because I'd be trying to get up on stage to stop Lukus from hurting you."

Brianna sighed. "Lukus won't hurt me, Tiff. Not really. Even today, he stopped and gave me a chance to regroup a couple of times during the punishment."

A feeling of uncertainty hit Tiffany. She leaned in even closer to her best friend, making double sure not to let their conversation be overheard. "But didn't it hurt?"

Bri leaned in closer with her answer. "God, yes.

It hurt like hell." Tiff could see Brianna remembering it as she reached back with both hands to rub her sore ass through the soft robe. Curious, Tiff was tempted to ask her friend to show her what her butt looked like after a dozen cane lashes but she stopped herself, afraid the sight might cause her to run screaming from the building.

If I had half a brain cell left, I'd have left long ago. Every minute I spend here, my ass gets closer to the fire.

"Then I don't get it, Bri. Help me understand. Why do you like it so much?"

"It's more than like. I don't know that I can explain it." Bri thought for a minute before continuing on. "Sometimes I just *need* to turn over control. Like today. It helped that he tied me down. Being immobile just sort of takes whatever happens out of my hands. I guess that's a big part of what I like. I love the feeling when I finally submit. It's liberating in a strange way."

Tiffany was quiet as she contemplated Bri's response. Before she could ask another question, she felt Lukus's strong hands grip her hips from behind as he stepped close. He was barely brushing his muscular chest against her back, but the slight contact caused her to shudder. She felt Lukus's lips brushing intimately against her ear as he leaned close to whisper to her.

"Baby, you left dinner unattended on the stove.

I was nice enough to turn it off for you this time, since I'm pretty sure you're not prepared for the stiff punishment I'd be forced to dish out if you tried to burn down my loft. Very naughty."

*Oh, my freaking God. Now I **know** I just totally creamed my panties.*

Tiffany knew she should have felt threatened by his words, but right that minute, all she really wanted to do was turn around, throw her arms around his neck, and beg him to take her right there on the damn kitchen counter.

Forcing herself to stay calm, she thanked him... *calmly.* "Thank you, Lukus. That was very nice of you."

Speaking a bit louder, he answered her. "Yes, it was nice if I do say so myself."

Tiff risked taking a quick peek over her shoulder and her eyes met the playful gaze of the Dom. The humor found there relaxed her right up to the point where he took a half-step away from her and smacked her ass with this open palm.

"Now get back in there and finish up. I'm starving."

She reflexively spun around, ready to give him a piece of her mind, but the words died on her lips as his eyes hungrily scanned her body. Tiffany couldn't miss the change in his breathing when he focused on her cleavage, as she was having trouble catching her own breath. It only got worse when she boldly allowed her own eyes to drift lower, taking in the large protrusion filling the front of his jeans.

A low moan actually escaped from Tiffany. Before she could even feel embarrassed, Lukus responded with his own low groan. It sounded like he was in pain and Tiff smiled when she realized he most likely *was* in pain with that hard-on squashed into those tight, sexy jeans all day.

Shit. Forget about creamed panties. I'm soaked now.

With a light giggle, Brianna stepped closer to the distracted couple, clearing her throat in an attempt to get their attention. "Lukus, I would really love to take a shower. If you don't mind, may I please use your bathroom?"

Without taking his eyes off Tiffany, he answered her distractedly. "Sure. Whatever."

Brianna looked back and forth between her two friends several times, before chuckling. "Have fun you two," she called as she headed to the bathroom. "Don't get so distracted you burn dinner."

Tiffany finally snapped out of her Lukus-induced trance just in time for Derek and Rachel to announce their departure, too. "Hey. We're going to get cleaned up in the guest room. We'll be back out in a little bit."

Tiffany glanced up in time to see Derek scooping his wife up in his arms to romantically carry her to the guest room. He stopped on the way out of the room to have a word with Lukus. Tiffany couldn't hear the conversation, only Derek's reply. "Sure thing. I'll take care of that right after I take care of Rachel."

Lukus laughed a knowing laugh. "Jesus Christ. You two fuck more than anyone else I know. Have fun. Just don't forget to take care of that before we need to head downstairs after dinner."

Tiffany wasn't used to people discussing their intention to have sex so blatantly. She'd been on the edge before, but only now did she realize her pussy was actually throbbing. Lucky for her, her head was stronger than her wayward girly parts. Before Lukus could close the distance between them again, she quickly sidestepped, heading back to the stove to relight the gas burners.

She worked hard to focus on the task at hand, but it wasn't easy. It got harder to ignore him when he took a seat on the stool directly across the island from her. Apparently, he wanted a front row seat to her cooking show. She should have felt safer with the wide island between them, but she wasn't foolish enough to think the granite expanse offered any kind of real protection from the Dom.

The first minute or two ticked by in quiet awkwardness. Now that they were alone again, it felt like all her assertiveness had deserted her to be replaced by a shy embarrassment. She went about browning the hamburger and chopping veggies for the sauce and salad, hoping to appear too busy to talk. But Lukus was on to her.

"So, are you planning on just ignoring me?"

She kept her eyes on the cutting board as she answered him with as steady a voice as she could muster. "Of course not. I'm not sure it would be possible to ignore you, Lukus. I'm just trying to finish dinner."

"I see that. But since you're stuck with me, at least for a little bit, maybe you should tell me something about yourself I should know."

Tiffany's heart jumped. She was confused about why he was trying to make small talk. She'd half expected him to pounce on her once they were alone and she tried to push down her confused disappointment at his gentlemanly demeanor. She glanced up as she replied. "Really? You're going the small talk route." Tiff was mad at herself when she heard the annoyance coming through in her tone.

"I never said it had to be small talk. You assumed that. Maybe I want you to tell me some deep dark secret." She looked up again to catch his devilish grin as she saw he was teasing her... egging her on.

"I think I'll keep all of my deep dark secrets to myself, thank you very much." Tiffany was running out of cooking tasks to make her look busy. She knew she was starting to look stupid by continuing to stir and stir the same pot unnecessarily. She suspected he'd noticed because when she finally aborted her stirring to look up again, he was staring at her.

"What?" she said nervously.

"I'm waiting. Tell me one thing you think will surprise me."

"Are you going to tell me something, too?"

He only hesitated a second before smiling. "Sure. Why not."

Her mind was racing to come up with something funny... clever... *non-sexual*. Tiff found her task harder than ever since right now, with him so close, she could hardly think of anything but sex. Finally, her mind blank, she gave up. "I truly can't think of a single thing right now."

"Really? That's curious. How about I make it easier on you then? I'll ask you one direct question and then you get to ask one of me. Kind of like truth or dare... only without the dare. You game?"

She knew she should decline. This was a very dangerous game to play with a man like Lukus. Still...

"I did say I was a good swimmer," she said. "I guess I'll take one question from the shark in the tank."

Lukus's grin was disarming. She suspected she was falling into a trap.

"Let's see. Such decisions. I think I'll go with a rather obvious question."

He paused dramatically and she could almost hear the drum roll. She was wary when his jovial expression was replaced with a smoldering, primal glare. "Tell me the truth... and I'll know if you're lying to me, Tiffany. After Bri, Derek, and Rachel left us alone, did you expect me to bend you over the counter and fuck you? Scratch that. When we were alone, did you *want* me to bend you over the counter and fuck you?"

OMG, I can feel the freaking juices dripping down my leg now, I'm so turned on. How could he know?

Her heart was racing so hard she heard the pounding in her ears. How in the world did she not see this coming? What the hell was she thinking, playing a game like this with such a dangerous man?

Now what? Do I tell him the truth? Will he be able to tell if I lie? How will I look him in the face if I tell him the truth?

The flood of internal questions continued as he patiently waited for her answer. When she opened her mouth, she was not really sure what was going to come out until she heard it for herself. She went with *less is more* and softly answered. "Yes."

His face lit up at her answer. Tiffany couldn't help but be glad she had told him the truth. A stray thought flitted through her racing brain that she might have considered walking over hot coals if it meant getting to see this sexy look on his face again. He was truly mesmerizing.

Tiffany finally woke up when she realized he was probably waiting for her to ask him a question. It was hard to concentrate when he was watching her so intently, especially now that he knew definitively she wanted him. The only lame question she could think of for the Dom was the obvious one, but she didn't need to waste her question asking if he wanted to bend her over the counter. His eyes and too-tight jeans had already answered that question long ago.

She finally cleared the cobwebs in her brain long enough to think of the question she most wanted an answer to. It was personal. It was perfect for this game. "My turn. Tell me Lukus... and I'll know if you're lying to me." She paused to put a twinkle in her eye as she parroted his prior warning back at him. "Have you ever had just a normal, vanilla relationship or have you always been in a D/s relationship?"

Only after the words left her mouth did Tiffany realize how truly important his answer was to this prying question. As hot as he was, she knew without a doubt she could not and would not ever turn into a 24/7 submissive. If that was what Lukus expected out of his relationships, it was better to know now and walk away without getting her heart —or other body parts—hurt. She'd worked hard to be an independent and strong businesswoman, and while her submissive tendencies where sex came in confused her, she knew that was where her line in the sand lay. She almost held her breath waiting for his answer.

He took his time. It was clear he was putting a

lot of thought into his answer. "That's not a simple yes/no question, now is it?"

Tiffany smiled. "I didn't know that was a prerequisite of the game."

"Touché." He shifted in his chair slightly, the only indication he was having trouble formulating his answer. On the surface, he was still the confident Dom she was just beginning to know and even respect. She wasn't sure how, but she instinctively knew whatever he said would be the truth.

"Well first, I think we need to define vanilla now, don't we? It's kind of like trying to define *normal*. What is vanilla to you?" He stopped long enough that Tiffany worried he was expecting her to answer, but he finally continued, much to her relief. "If by vanilla you mean being in a relationship where I have sex once a week, missionary style, in a bed with the lights off... well then, no. I can't say that type of relationship has ever interested me."

Before she could stop and think, Tiffany blurted back. "Oh, thank God. Because that sounds awful."

Lukus laughed out loud at her outburst. She felt herself turning beet red. Thankfully he didn't make her elaborate before he continued on. "Listen, I know what you're asking and truthfully, I haven't been in many, what most people would call, *relationships* at all. But when I have been in a monogamous relationship, it's always been with someone who had submissive tendencies, yes." He was watching her carefully. It was clear he was gauging her reaction.

"Define tendencies."

"Tiffany, this lifestyle isn't black and white. Everyone has his or her own limits, their own list of turn-ons and turn-offs. And our limits tend to change over time. I know I'm not looking for the same things today I was even five years ago when I opened the club."

His frankness caught her off guard. It sounded like there was a lot more he wanted to say. She wanted to ask it, the question hanging in the air unsaid. She couldn't resist. "What *are* you looking for, Lukus?"

He didn't even hesitate with his answer. It was as if he was just waiting patiently for her to ask. "I want more. Truthfully, I'm not even sure exactly what that means, but I know that being the Master of Many, as Derek likes to call me, just isn't making me happy anymore."

Tiffany noticed the slightest of changes in the confident Dom. It wasn't obvious, but she detected a new vulnerability in him, and she realized he'd just shared something very private with her. While his statement was somewhat cryptic, she understood enough to suspect he didn't disclose his feelings with many other people. The conversation was getting too personal. She felt flushed. "Well, your secret is safe with me, Lukus."

A feeling of relief settled over the kitchen. They both seemed satisfied enough with their new tidbits of personal information to fall into an easy, lighthearted conversation. They spent the next fifteen minutes discussing their favorite movies, music, and TV shows while Tiffany mixed up the brownies and put the pasta on to cook. She was having so much fun, she totally forgot she was supposed to be guarding herself from him.

CHAPTER ELEVEN

LUKUS

Lukus couldn't believe how much fun he was having doing nothing more than simply chatting with Tiffany as she cooked dinner. They enjoyed discussing the pros and cons of chick-flicks vs. action movies. He loved the surprise on her face when he let it slip that he had a movie theater in the loft. She immediately begged him to take her for a tour after dinner and he had to push down the urge to start the tour now. It was ludicrous that he was thrilled at the thought of sharing this space, his home, with her. He tried not to get distracted by over-analyzing his own feelings.

Don't question it, Mitchell. Just relax and go for the ride.

Just as that thought flitted through his consciousness, he heard Tiffany telling him to set the table. Out of habit, Lukus's first instinct was to lash out at her.

How dare she order me to do something? I'm in charge here. It's my loft, for Christ's sake.

Tiffany's whole demeanor changed as she watched him closely, waiting to see how he was going to react to her request. A small smile played on her lips and he suspected she'd made her request to test him. Well, he'd be damned if he was going to fall into her trap.

"Sure. No problem," he answered stiffly. Lukus went about setting five places at the large eat-in island. When he was done, he walked to the well-stocked wine rack and took down a bottle along with glasses from the near-by stemware rack. Once he had the bottle open, he took it all to the table before detouring to the refrigerator to grab the carton of milk. He saw Tiffany watching him curiously as he carried the carton to the table and began to fill one of the five wine glasses with milk instead of wine. Looking up at her confusion, he simply clarified. "Rachel."

Tiffany nodded. "Right. Hey, where do you keep your strainer or colander for the pasta?"

"It's in the cabinet above the microwave."

"Okay, thanks."

Lukus stood back, watching as Tiff headed to collect the colander, knowing that *he* had trouble reaching it. It was really high. He liked the nice view of her bare, toned legs as her dress hiked up on the right side as she lifted her arm high, trying to reach the colander. When she unexpectedly wheeled around, she caught him ogling her. She smiled knowingly, her hands on her hips, before prodding him. "Well, don't just stand there. You know I'm never gonna be able to reach it."

Such sass.

It was completely foreign to him how both Brianna and Tiffany talked to him in their unguarded moments. He was so used to submissives and even full-time slaves around him who would rather cut off their right arm than talk to him with such a tone. The powerful feelings their total submission and accompanying anxiety produced by being pushed out of their comfort zone used to be intoxicating to him. He assumed in the right situation, it still would be.

But here in his kitchen, making dinner with this beautiful blonde with her to-die-for body, he realized what was turning him on more than anything else was her fearless ability to go toe-to-toe with him. She had fire. He knew he wanted to be careful not to douse that fire completely.

Assuming he wasn't coming to her aide, Tiffany had returned to the futile task of retrieving the colander. Lukus couldn't resist the opportunity to come up behind her, pressing her body between his and the kitchen counter. He could hear her sharp intake of breath when his fully erect cock pressed hard against her lower back. He knew it wasn't playing fair, but he ground his hips ever so slightly to make sure she understood the full effect she was having on him. He reached up to capture the wayward strainer but didn't step away from her right away. Instead, he set the strainer down and moved to wrap his arms around her waist, pulling her fully against him. Burying his face in her hair, Lukus took a deep drag of her heavenly scent.

You'd better be careful, Mitchell. You're about to cross a line. Markus... think about Markus.

Tiffany's whimper as she pushed her ass backwards against his tortured tool caused his control to slip further. His mouth found the sensitive skin where her neck met bare shoulder. As if he needed any more sexual stimulation, the first taste of her skin was like an aphrodisiac. The quick kiss soon turned into an all-out, open mouth, licking, and sucking up and down the sensitive skin of her neck. He didn't even try to stop from sucking hard enough to leave a mark. He *wanted* them both to have evidence he'd been there.

Lukus could feel her continuing to grind back against him, her breathing ragged. He could smell the evidence of her arousal wafting up from between her legs and he let his left hand slowly slide down her body to stroke her through her dress and panties. The second his fingers reached the apex between her legs, her entire body shuddered under his touch. She threw her head back to rest against his shoulder. He could feel her legs give out from under her as a powerful orgasm wracked her body. Only his strong embrace was holding her upright now and he was literally in danger of shooting his cum into his pants. She reached back with both hands to grasp his hips, helping to hold them tightly together.

Jesus Christ. What the hell was that? It took all of sixty-seconds of fully clothed groping to make her come. Don't you dare embarrass yourself by shooting it right now. Hold it, Mitchell.

Lukus was smart enough to stop the grinding and Tiffany was too lost in her post-orgasm high to keep pulling him closer. They remained locked in their embrace, each of them trying to get control before they had to face each other again. This was exactly how Brianna found them upon her return to the kitchen.

"Oh shit. I'm so sorry, you guys. I'll come back later."

Waking up from his trance, Lukus made sure Tiffany could now support her own weight before releasing her and taking a step backwards. There was no hiding his raging hard-on from anyone who cared to look. He worked hard to steady his voice when he answered her. "No problem, Brianna. You can stay. I was just helping Tiffany get the strainer down for the pasta."

"Yeah... right."

He risked a quick glance her way and saw a knowing smile plastered all over her face. He decided it was best to just ignore her taunt. He was literally saved by the bell when the buzzer announced it was time to take the brownies out of the oven. He managed to hide his precarious condition by walking away from the girls to tend to the dessert. Lukus spent a couple long minutes willing his manhood to take a nap since it was definitely not time to come out and play.

They somehow managed to gloss over the first few awkward moments and by the time Derek and Rachel rejoined them for dinner, everything seemed back to normal. As the strange mix of new and old friends got to know each other better over wine and food, Lukus took a minute to reflect on how quickly things could change in life. Little more than twenty-four hours ago, he hadn't even met Brianna, let alone Tiffany. He'd been plotting with his best friend to punish his wayward wife properly. Now here he was, actually enjoying the spontaneous dinner party.

A sense of foreboding washed over him as he thought about Markus and tonight's continued punishment plan for Brianna. He had no idea when he had come up with the plan how much he would become personally invested in the results of tonight's events. It was rare for him to feel apprehensive before a scene; usually he was excited. But now he was suddenly afraid of what both he and Markus might have to lose if things didn't go as planned. He looked at his watch and saw that the time was getting close.

Don't be such a pussy. You're the Dom. The plan is solid. Suck it up and get going.

His fingers collided with Tiffany's as they both reached for one of last two brownies left on the plate. Lukus swatted her fingers away. "Hey, you've already had your share. This last edge one is all mine. I don't like the center ones."

"Wait. Neither do I. Brianna always lets me have the edges. You take the center one."

"Oh no you don't. You take the center one."

Only then did it hit Lukus that he was sitting in his kitchen actually *enjoying* battling with Tiff over a fucking brownie. Diving into completely uncharted territory, Lukus picked up the center brownie and was immediately rewarded with a victorious grin lighting up Tiffany's face that made it all worth it.

You're so fucking screwed, man.

Tiffany

The girls were just finishing cleaning up the kitchen when the men came back to the loft. They'd left right after the group had finished dessert. The mood during dinner had been jovial, and Tiffany was on cloud nine. She'd discovered so much about Lukus in such a short period of time, and what she'd learned only made her want to learn more. Her original worries about him being a menacing Dom like Jake had all but evaporated, and she found herself almost giddy at the prospect of spending more time with him. Oddly, she wasn't even embarrassed by the fact she'd orgasmed so easily. He had a magic touch and knew how to push her buttons—literally.

But now, as they returned from wherever it was they'd gone, her anxiety returned. Gone were the light-hearted expressions. Both men's faces were now set in stern dominance. The shift in the atmosphere was immediate and staggering for the women. All three reacted in their own way.

Rachel gracefully lowered herself to her knees, legs spread wide, her palms up on her thighs, eyes diverted downward, waiting for direction.

Brianna's face projected fear. Her best friend had confided her dread of the continued punishment, but Bri was determined to do anything to win her husband's trust back. If that included another humiliating and painful punishment session on stage with Lukus tonight, then her friend was determined to survive it for Markus and her marriage.

Tiffany knew it was ironic that she probably felt the most afraid, even though she had no actual punishment coming. Of course, part of her fear was for her best friend. She worried about Bri getting hurt again, like she had with Jake. While she knew

Lukus would never let that happen, she couldn't help but feel apprehension.

But if she was honest with herself, her biggest fear was just seeing this change in Lukus and knowing this was a big part of who he was. While he'd been flirtatious and even tender with her at dinner, looking at him now reminded her he was a Dominant, through and through. She was a fool if she thought he was going to just walk away from this part of his life like Markus had done for Bri. The realization filled her with a sense of loss... loss for something she'd never really had, but had glimpsed for just a few short minutes at dinner.

He's a Dom... and you're not a submissive. This is never going to work and you're a fool to ever think it could.

She noticed Lukus avoided looking her way as he took control of the scene. "Brianna and Rachel, strip... *now*."

Bri and Tiffany exchanged a quick glance before Brianna slowly slipped the soft robe from her body, letting it pool at her feet. Standing behind her friend, Tiffany got her first glimpse at the welts across Bri's butt and legs where she'd been caned. Even now, hours later, the stripes were clearly visible. Tiff's heart lurched at the mere thought of surviving something like a caning and her eyes involuntarily sought out Lukus's. She was unnerved to find him watching her, taking in her reaction. If he was upset by the anger he must have seen dancing in her eyes, he hid it well.

"The show is about to start. I need you girls to go down with Derek. Brianna, he's going to prepare you for your punishment center stage tonight."

"Oh, God. Please, not that Sir. Can't you punish me backstage?"

"No and you know better than to even ask me. Go. I need to talk to Tiffany for a few minutes. I'll meet you downstairs."

Derek reached out a hand to pull his wife to her feet, leaving her robe behind on the floor. "Come on you naughty girls. Let's get you downstairs."

Only as they were walking away did Tiffany see the thick, cherry red stripes left on Rachel's ass and legs. When the others were on the elevator, she looked back to see Lukus watching her again. She was about to blow. "I can't believe this is what you do for a living, Lukus. Seriously. How many nights a week do you do this? How many women have you punished over your lifetime? And how many of them ended up here fixing you spaghetti just like I did? What a fucking fool I was. I actually forgot for a while what you do for kicks on a Saturday night. Well, I'm never going—"

Lukus had had enough. He quickly closed the gap between them and yanked her to him, clamping his hand over her mouth to shush her. "Enough. Settle down, baby."

Tiffany fought free of his hand, but wasn't strong enough to get away from his grasp. "Don't you dare 'baby' me. I can't believe you."

"Listen. I haven't lied to you. Like it or not, this is part of who I am. I have a job to do tonight. I'm gonna walk you down to your car now and you're going to drive home and stay there until Brianna calls you. Do you hear me?"

She must have heard him wrong. "What? You actually think for one minute I'd ever willingly leave Brianna here to be terrorized by you and Derek again? No way! It's bad enough Markus deserted her, leaving her here to go through all of this alone—even knowing the hell she's been through at the hands of Jake. Markus is such a chicken shit. He should be here taking care of his wife on his own instead of wimping out on his duties as her husband."

Lukus took a deep breath. "I don't disagree with you on that count, but the fact remains that tonight is a club event and you aren't a member of the club." Releasing her from his embrace, he kept a grip on her upper arm as he started to shuffle them along towards the elevator. "You need to go home now, Tiffany. I don't want you here tonight."

Tiffany saw an almost pained look cross his face and for a brief moment, she caught a glimpse of the tender Lukus she'd had so much fun bantering with earlier. He was a complicated man.

They were almost to the elevator when Tiffany

tried to break away. "I mean it. I'm not leaving. You can drag my ass down to my car and even put me in it, but you can't make me drive away, Lukus. I'm going to just sit out in the alley until Brianna is ready to go home. I'm not leaving my best friend behind."

Lukus looked like he was about to blow. "Fuck. You're an infuriating woman, do you know that, Tiffany... Shit, I don't even know your last name."

"Why the hell do you care what my last name is?"

"Humor me."

"No." Tiff crossed her arms across her chest in defiance.

"Fuck it. I'm a private investigator. I can get everything from your shoe size to your first-grade teacher from a damn computer with a lot less hassle than you're giving me right now, little girl. Come on. You're going home."

When she started to slap his hands away, the Dom had had enough. He yanked her to him so they were face-to-face. His green eyes were almost black with anger. An involuntary shiver shook Tiffany, but she refused to look away from him. As their standoff continued, Tiffany saw a new resolve washing over his handsome face. "So... you've decided you want to stay to see what happens to Brianna. You won't leave without her, is that it?"

"You can force me out of the building, but I'm not leaving without her, Lukus."

"It's not safe for you out in the alley."

"Then let me stay up here."

Lukus looked conflicted. Tiffany suspected her defiance was pushing him harder than anyone had ever pushed before. She wasn't backing down. Finally, he made up his mind. "Fine, but I'm telling you here and now that you're asking for this. I warned you. I want you to leave. If you don't like what you end up seeing tonight, well, that's on you. Do you hear me?" When Tiff didn't answer fast enough, he shook her. "Do you?"

"Yes, Lukus. You're off the hook. It's on me," she spat.

He didn't look very placated. His scolding tone of voice confirmed. "Stand right here and don't you dare move a muscle. Can you do that or are you going to argue with me on this too?"

Tiffany couldn't stop the small smile. "Yes. I think I can manage."

Lukus disappeared into his bedroom and came out just a minute or two later carrying a small duffle bag over his shoulder. He looked like he was heading out to the gym. When he got near, he surprised her by reaching out to grab her hand, entwining their fingers. She was stunned at the simple intimacy of his touch and almost forgot to start walking along with him towards the elevator. As they waited for the doors to open, she got nervous wondering what she'd gotten herself into.

As the elevator doors closed and they were

headed downstairs, she voiced her worry. "Please don't tell me you're planning to put me in the audience to watch this. Please, let me stay upstairs... or I'll wait for you in your office. You can't expect me to watch this."

"I warned you. You made your choice. I can't trust you to stay up there or in the office. I need to know where you're going to be tonight and if I can't know you're safe at your house, then I'm going to park you in a different place where I know without a doubt you'll stay safe... and quiet... and out of the way."

Tiffany didn't have time to evaluate this new information because they'd stopped on the second floor. The elevator doors opened to a very dark and narrow hallway. She'd only been on the first and seventh floors up until now. This floor was dark and scary and she worried he may be planning on locking her in a dungeon. The farther down the long hallway they got, the slower she walked and the more he had to drag her along behind him by their still-linked hands.

Finally, the hallway widened and they started to pass a series of closed doors with numbers on them. The doors counted down from six and when they arrived at the door labeled with a one, there was a circular staircase winding down to the ground floor. Tiffany curiously followed Lukus down the stairs and she found herself in what looked like the lobby of an old-fashioned grand theater. She took in the curtain-draped walls and marble floors. She could hear loud music playing from the other side of the security door.

Lukus stopped just before the door and turned to her. "Last chance, Tiff. It's not too late. I can walk you to your car."

Tiffany was actually tempted this time. She really didn't want to watch her best friend go through a punishment like a caning, belting, or— God forbid—another punishment enema. She pushed her fear down, knowing she couldn't leave Bri here alone. "I'm staying, Lukus."

"Suit yourself. I warned you."

Lukus turned and put in a six-digit code that opened the door, allowing entry to the main floor of The Punishment Pit. Tiffany had been preparing herself to see Doms and naked submissives waiting for the show to start. Brianna had described the scene to Tiff when they talked earlier so she was pretty sure she knew what to expect. Her eyes sought out Lukus's. "Where is everybody? I thought you said the show was about to begin."

He grinned. "Let's just say we're going to have a private show tonight. You'll be the only audience member in attendance."

He didn't give her a chance to question him. He was walking towards the comfortable seating areas closer to center stage. Lukus looked around as if he was trying to decide something before dragging over a specific chair from a neighboring sitting arrangement. It had to be the most uncomfortable-looking chair in the house. It looked to be a simple side chair from a dining room set, but with a cushioned seat. He steered Tiffany to sit down. Then he knelt at her feet and opened the gym bag.

She couldn't help but let out a protesting yelp when she saw the items he started to pull from the bag. She was smart enough to keep her mouth closed as she watched him attaching the wide leather ankle cuffs to each of her legs. He produced a length of rope and used it to secure her legs to either side of the chair. By the time he was done, her lower half was immobilized, her legs splayed wide open.

She was grateful he left her dress on, but felt a rush of embarrassment when she realized even she could smell her lingering arousal. She saw the small smile cross Lukus's handsome face and she was pretty sure he could smell it, too.

Lukus moved to her arms next. Tiffany forced herself to remain calm and quiet, reminding herself she'd chosen this. Okay, maybe not exactly *this*, but even if she'd known he was going to tie her down, it still wouldn't have made her want to leave Bri behind alone. It only took him a minute to put on the wrist cuffs and then pull her arms behind the chair where he tied her wrists to the ropes securing her ankles. She was now completely immobile.

"Are you comfortable enough? The ropes aren't cutting into you, are they?"

She was grateful for his concern. "No, they're fine. I'm wishing I'd gone to the bathroom before we came down, but I can hold it."

"Okay, I'll be back after the show ends. I have one more thing to add to your ensemble and I know you're not going to like it, but it's necessary. You can cuss me out later if you still want to."

Before Tiff could even guess what he was talking about, he reached into the gym bag and pulled out what at first glance looked like a red bouncy ball. It only took a split second to realize it had straps attached and he intended to gag her with this huge ball gag. Their eyes met and she saw regret in his eyes. He reached out as she opened her mouth to protest to shove the red ball into her mouth. Tiff was furious and her anger grew when she realized just how big the damn thing was. It started to feel uncomfortable almost immediately and she was grateful it at least had a little give so she could bite down.

"I'm sorry about how big this is, Tiff. I know it's too big for you as a beginner, but I didn't have any others upstairs. I'll look backstage and if I have time, I'll bring a smaller one out. I know this doesn't make sense to you, but I can't have you interfering with Brianna's punishment tonight. I warned you. I know you're not going to like what you're going to see, and I just can't have her being able to hear you out here, baby."

She wanted to scream at him to stop calling her baby, but it only came out as a jumbled gurgle behind the gag. She could already feel drool pooling in her mouth and knew it was only a matter of time before it tried to escape to run down her chin. Lukus stood and stepped back, taking a minute to admire his handy-work. The look on his face was a strange mix of predator and protector, each battling with the other. It looked like the protector won out when he stepped forward to stroke her cheek gently, cupping it tenderly while he leaned down to place a kiss on her forehead. His lips remained there for several long seconds before he pulled away. "Be a good girl now, baby. I'll be back for you after the show."

Tiff had to watch him as he turned and headed up the stairs center stage. He found the split where the stage curtains met and with a last quick glance her way, disappeared behind the curtain, leaving her alone with her thoughts in the expansive theater.

You just wait, Lukus Mitchell. I'm so going to get even with you for this. I'll teach you. Not every woman wants to be treated like a damn submissive.

The thought was barely complete when she felt the throbbing in her pussy returning. Clearly her private parts hadn't gotten the memo that they weren't supposed to like this kind of treatment.

CHAPTER TWELVE

TIFFANY

Tiffany spent her first few minutes alone trying to calm her ragged nerves and get a handle on her conflicted emotions. She was furious with Lukus for tying her down and forcing her to witness her best friend's humiliating punishment. Regardless of the blackmail, she was angry with Brianna for cheating on Markus with that asshole Jake and putting herself in danger yet again. She was disgusted with Markus and his inability to be man enough to come deal with his wife himself. And, she was terrified of what she was going to be forced to watch tonight, yet a small part of her was almost excited to see Lukus in all of his Dom glory. That excitement, in turn, led her to her strongest emotion of all—confusion. Conflicting emotions warred inside her, making her feel like she had a split personality. Strait-laced Tiffany who'd grown up in a strict Catholic family warred with the sexually liberated version of herself who'd somehow tapped into deep desires she had no way of verbalizing.

I can't believe how easily I fell for him. I actually had an orgasm in his kitchen, for Christ's sake. Have you no pride, Tiffany?

In her confusion, Tiffany wanted to scream at him to come release her from her bindings—to stay furious at him for tying her up and gagging her. This wasn't supposed to be part of the deal. Only after several panicked minutes did she realize she had to let go of the anger, knowing it was futile to waste her energy.

Lukus won't let me go. Not until he's good and ready. And he's definitely not ready.

Tiff closed her eyes, letting the techno beat of the dance music pump through her veins. She recalled how Brianna described the liberation that came from being restrained, or surrendering to punishment. At the time, Tiffany hadn't really connected with what her friend was saying. But now, despite her, or maybe because of her precarious position, Tiffany felt her own submissive feelings stirring, clearing through the cloud of confusion.

She focused on how helpless she felt and within a few short minutes of inner reflection, she found she'd made the tricky journey from sassy to submissive. It scared her how easily she allowed the feeling of surrender to settle in. With her body immobilized, her intuition felt more alive, more aware of every nuance of her body—the stretch of her immobilized muscles, the throbbing of her pussy as it remembered Lukus's touch, the ache of her wide-open mouth. The latter made her think of how wonderful it would be if Lukus would come replace the ball gag with that oversized cock she'd been admiring through his jeans.

Maybe it was because of what she'd been exposed to over the last few hours, but she didn't just want to give Lukus a simple blowjob. No. She wanted him to face-fuck her, to use her helpless mouth as repayment for the orgasm he'd already given her. She knew something revolutionary had changed in her when she even recognized she actually *wanted* him to come in her mouth and force her to swallow every last drop of his warm cum. She'd traditionally been a no-swallow kind of girl. Yet, here, tonight she found she wanted anything and everything that sexy man could dish out.

Tiff wasn't sure how long she waited there, splayed open and tied immobile to the chair, but it was long enough for the drool to begin spilling out on both sides of the too-big red gag in her mouth. She should have been embarrassed at the loss of such a simple body function, but it only enhanced her feeling of surrender. Her limbs were stiff, and her bladder beginning to feel the pressure. Why wasn't Lukus checking on her?

She was about to doze off when she heard a commotion on the other side of the curtains. The lights where Tiffany was located suddenly went out, throwing the entire club into complete darkness. It only lasted a few seconds before new music started pumping louder, signaling the start of the show. Within a minute, the curtains began to open slowly, revealing the dimly lit secrets held behind them.

Tiffany had tried to prepare herself mentally for what she would see, but it was quickly clear she'd failed miserably. Nothing could have prepared her for this.

Brianna was naked, center stage. Her arms were stretched high above her head and spread wide apart, secured by leather wrist cuffs to two hooks hanging down from the rafters. From the angle her friend was facing, Tiffany knew she'd be able to see every expression that crossed her face during punishment. She suspected Lukus staged it this way on purpose.

Bri's ankle cuffs were anchored to hooks in the floor, spreading her legs wide. Lukus had brought in what looked like a pommel horse, similar to those used in gymnastics, sans the handgrips. He had it positioned in front of Brianna's waist. Her arms had been pulled forward on the ceiling enough so that she was being forced to lean forward over the horse. The position left her most private parts completely exposed, vulnerable, and available for punishment.

Brianna was also blindfolded; she'd be unable to see any of the punishments coming beforehand.

Only now did Tiffany understand why Lukus had gagged her. Without a doubt, she would have been screaming at him to let Brianna go. The indignant anger she'd been successfully suppressing now resurfaced with a vengeance.

How dare he do this to Brianna? How dare he do this to me?

The music started to get a bit softer, and Tiff heard Derek announcing the start of tonight's show as he introduced Master Lukus Mitchell, Master of Masters. Lukus burst onto the stage, pumped up and looking ready for battle. Tiffany had never seen him like this—wearing his Dom persona as if it were a well-tailored suit. He looked so powerful— beautifully dangerous. A strong wave of dread washed over her.

What the hell was I thinking? This guy is hardcore. He's not the kind of man who's going to be interested in playing house with me out in the suburbs. I need to get away from him the instant he lets me loose, even if I have to leave Brianna behind.

Tiffany snapped her eyes closed, desperate to shut out the scene on stage. She knew she had no choice but to somehow get through watching Lukus punish Brianna. She only hoped she could make it through without getting turned on like in the past when watching punishments of strangers at the clubs she used to go to with Bri, or when reading about similar punishment scenes in the *Beauty* books.

When several minutes passed and she heard nothing new, she finally opened her eyes to see Lukus standing near the front of the stage, staring at her. He'd been waiting for her to open her eyes, as if he didn't want her to miss a single minute of the upcoming torture. She didn't try to hide her fury. He might have restrained her body, but Tiffany made it clear by the daggers in her eyes that her mind was still her own.

Fuck you, Lukus Mitchell. You've pushed me too far. I'm done swimming in your shark tank, buddy.

If Lukus could detect her defiance, he wasn't rattled by it. He stood planted, staring at her—admiring her—*consuming* her. Tiffany's heart raced faster as his gaze drew her in against her will. Just when the electric current peaked, Lukus broke into his sexy smile—the smile she'd vowed to crawl over hot coals to see again.

Well, fuck me. I guess I can tread water for a bit longer.

Brianna

W *hat is he waiting for?*
A shudder raced through Brianna's whole body from the convergence of fear, humiliation, guilt, and excited anticipation.

Brianna wasn't entirely sure what was going on. She'd spent thirty minutes backstage before finally being brought out front for the start of the show. She should've been relieved when Derek had simply parked both women in Lukus's office while he worked on the computer. While Rachel had looked quite content to kneel patiently silent by Derek's feet, Brianna had wanted to crawl out of her skin. With the promise of her impending punishment in front of the Saturday night crowd hanging over her head, there was little to do but imagine all the wicked things Lukus might have been cooking up for tonight.

She'd finally forced herself to calm down by reminding herself all that she had learned over the last twenty-four hours. Tonight, felt totally different than last night. One of the most important things she'd learned was that Lukus would never hurt her. Not really. In her reflection time at Derek's feet, she'd finally submitted to the notion she'd just have to trust him.

But she'd almost wavered when Lukus burst into the office in an obvious state of agitation. She still had no clue what had gotten him so upset, but he'd been rummaging through drawers and cabinets looking for something before spending five minutes yelling at Derek for letting their stock of extra toys dwindle to an unacceptable selection. She'd had no clue what they were really referring to; she was just relieved that for once, he wasn't pissed at her. She'd had a pretty strong inclination, though, that Tiffany might have been at the heart of his foul mood this time.

You go, girl. He deserves everything you can dish out.

Brianna could have kicked herself when she'd unwittingly walked into the kitchen earlier to catch her friend red handed in an intimate embrace. They'd been facing away from her, so she wasn't completely sure what had transpired, but there'd been an undeniable electric current passing between the two of them all night during dinner. She'd truly enjoyed watching the dynamic as the Master of Masters and reluctant sub felt each other out.

How awesome would that be if Lukus and Tiffany got together?

She suspected they were both going to resist the pull, thinking they were from two different worlds, but Brianna knew enough about them both to know they were perfect for each other. If she ever dug herself out of this punishment hell she'd cast herself into, she was going to do her best to play matchmaker.

The ache in her shoulders brought Brianna

back to the here and now. With each passing minute she became more confused. When Lukus had announced it was time to go front-of-house, he'd helped pull her to her feet before escorting her out to center stage. She'd been relieved the heavy curtains had been drawn, keeping the hungry audience at bay for at least a few more minutes.

The dance music was playing even louder tonight than last night, making any real conversation in the club almost impossible. It hadn't bothered her as it gave her and Lukus a legitimate reason to remain silent while he'd gone about the business of preparing her for her public punishment session. She'd quickly realized how silly she'd been to hold out hope he might go easy on her tonight now that they felt more like friends.

Lukus had methodically reattached her wrist and ankle cuffs first. Then, like a true artist, had gone about his craft of immobilizing her in an almost artful and creative display of submission and vulnerability. Her arms were pulled high, her legs spread wide as they were attached to rings in the floor. She surely would have tipped over in the precarious position were it not for the pommel horse placed strategically in front of her, the top at perfect waist-height.

Only once he'd had the horse in place did Brianna realize the hooks her arms were attached to were part of a mechanically controlled system. Lukus had used a remote control to move her arms forward a foot or so, just enough to force her feet uncomfortably onto her tippy toes and her tummy to lean across the horse. While it felt good to let some of her weight be supported by the horse, Bri had recognized immediately that she was in the most compromising position possible. Her sore ass and wet pussy were exposed, both now perfect targets for any implement in his extensive arsenal. Her heavy breasts were now being pulled away from her body slightly by gravity, making them targets as well.

The blindfold had been harder to take.

"Sorry, sweetheart," Lukus had said. "But I think it'll be easier on you tonight if you can't see what's coming next."

Brianna had wanted to argue with him, but instead simply thanked him. "Yes, Sir. Thank you, Sir."

He'd leaned in to brush his lips across her forehead in a chaste kiss.

"Be a good girl tonight Brianna. You know you need to be punished for hurting Markus, but know I'll never really hurt you. Stay true to yourself and everything will be just fine."

Then he'd left her alone with her thoughts and fears until she heard the announcement starting the show.

And here she was, waiting. During last night's show Lukus had addressed the audience at length. Tonight, he'd barely done any talking at all. Still, having only been here one night, she had no clue if this was normal. She felt so vulnerable, splayed out like this for the audience, and she felt a sudden gratitude both for the blindfold and the music that was blocking it all out. At least this way she had a small chance of forgetting there was a roomful of spectators only feet away witnessing her humiliation and punishment.

As much as she dreaded the punishment, the waiting was worse. She wanted him to just get it over with. She was somewhat relieved when she heard Lukus finally address the audience, reminding them he'd been charged with punishing his best friend's wife for her infidelity.

"I've spent the last twenty-four hours punishing the little adulteress just like she deserved. She's had everything from whippings, beltings, and canings, to punishment enemas and painful, personal exams. Still, she's refused to sign the papers granting her husband a divorce. I have to tell you all that, against my better judgment, I'm beginning to admire her resolve to save her marriage. Regardless, I have a job to do and that job is to continue to punish her for her unforgivable behavior."

His sudden touch on her breast was unexpected. She'd been on pins and needles expecting pain, so the gentle caress molding and squeezing first one and then the other breast caught Brianna completely off guard.

"Lukus, what the hell are you doing?"

Her answer came in the form of a hard swat against her breast, just catching her nipple and sending shock waves of pain and pleasure through her.

"Excuse me? What is my name during a punishment?"

"Sir," she corrected herself. "I'm so sorry Sir, but why are you touching me like this?"

"I don't think that's any of your concern. I'll punish you—use you—any way I choose to and if you're truly ready to make amends, you'll accept that punishment gratefully as your atonement to Markus."

Brianna's mind was racing. While it was true she'd certainly felt a draw to Lukus's strength, and had even reveled in the scorching hot kiss they had shared in his bed this afternoon, she was sure they were well past the danger of giving into their base attraction to each other, if not for their own sakes, then for Markus. Yet here he was, clearly confusing her by intimately touching her body.

The pain from the slap to her breast had subsided when she felt it—Lukus's warm mouth sucking her left tit as if he were nursing from her. Before she could rein the feeling in, a shudder of pleasure raced through her. A low moan escaped as she felt him licking and lightly sucking on her sensitive nipple. It was the nip of his teeth that finally woke her up.

"Sir, stop it right now. What the hell are you… OWEEE!!!"

The pain was sudden and excruciating. Without her eyesight, she could only go by touch, but it felt as if he'd just clamped a heavy-duty, tightly pinching nipple clamp onto her now hard nipple. The pain was exquisite and shot a direct line of stimulation to her throbbing sex. The pain hadn't settled in yet when she felt that insistent mouth drawing on her other nipple. Now, knowing what was coming, Brianna tried to let the pleasure she was feeling from his warm mouth calm her enough to help power through the pain she knew was soon to follow.

The feel of Lukus's mouth on her, sucking and nipping her pink nub was intoxicating. Her inability to stop him enhanced her feeling of submission. Yet her brain fought the feeling that this was wrong. It was too personal.

"Sir, why are you doing this? Markus wouldn't want you touching me like this." She was saying all the right words, but even she could hear her lack of commitment to her chastity. She'd been horny all afternoon and the feel of his warm mouth on her made her want more. Regardless, he finally did tear his warm mouth away from her nipple, quickly replacing it with the other clamp. She was somewhat ready for it this time so when the clamp pinched her nub tightly, only a low groan escaped her lips. Her nipples were numbing from the clamps until she felt Lukus attaching heavy weights to first one and then the other, letting his fingers graze the tender tips.

She was surprised when he spoke softly in her ear, his lips so close she could feel his whiskers brush her cheek. "You really like this, don't you sweetheart? I suspected you would. You like being tied up, helpless... tortured and on display."

"Oh no, Sir. It hurts so much. Please, take the clamps off."

"Tsk... tsk... tsk. You shouldn't lie to your Master, naughty girl. You know I can always tell when a submissive isn't being truthful."

"It hurts too much. Please, I'm begging you." Bri could the hear panic in her own voice as she fought to get the burn of pain under control.

"Tell me. The pain is turning you on, isn't it Brianna? Never mind. You don't need to answer me with words. I have my own, foolproof way of finding the truth."

Brianna was finally getting her breathing under control from the pain in her nipples when she felt Lukus's hand slowly caressing her welted ass, kneading it, slowly and sensuously. It was as if he were admiring his earlier handiwork.

Lukus slowly slipped his fingers lower, stroking her wet slit several times before dipping at least two digits deep into her cunt. While the sensation felt wonderful, Brianna was mortified at the wet slurp as he stroked her and she cried out.

"Oh God, no. Please, not there. I need to come so bad Sir, but not like this. I need to be a good girl and wait for Markus to forgive me."

She was relieved when Lukus chuckled and removed his invading digits. "Good girl. That's the right answer, sweetheart."

She briefly reveled in the glow of his approval. She smelled the evidence of her arousal just before she felt his wet fingers pressing against her lips, demanding entry. She hungrily opened her mouth to suck her own juices from his digits. It felt so decadent to be enjoying her own taste as he spent several long seconds finger-fucking her mouth until all traces of her essence were cleaned away.

He stepped away and a few seconds later she felt the sting of what she suspected was a riding crop landing across the top of her already tortured breasts. The pain was all consuming and only the restraints kept her in place. She was unable to defend herself from the next onslaught. She didn't have long to wait. The next swing came from the opposite direction, catching the tender underside of her breasts hard and strong.

"Ohhhhhhh noooooo! Oh, God!" She was panting in an attempt to power through the pain.

While the first two swings of the riding crop had been strategically spread out, the next half dozen strikes came fast and furious, never giving Bri a chance to catch her breath. She was a bawling, mumbling mess by the time the strikes stopped coming. She vaguely had to acknowledge that as bad as the pain was, taking the strokes on her recently caned bottom would have been worse. So, when that was what happened, her screams let Lukus know the punishment was doing its job.

Brianna began to release the final shred of control she'd been clinging to as the next thwack of the crop connected with her most tender spot where her butt and thighs met, dragging a guttural cry from her.

She felt it starting and she was certain that Lukus had to recognize the signs as well. His well-placed last strike had set her on her way to her happy place. Her brain knew she was supposed to push the feelings down, but all willpower was gone. With each masterful stroke of the crop, she flew higher and higher.

She was waiting for something. Oh yes... waiting for him to warn her... to stop her from coming as he had several times today, but when his warning didn't come, she took his silence as his tacit approval.

Her powerful orgasm erupted with the next strike to her welted breasts. The torturous end of the crop connected like a bullseye with one of her clamped nips. The pain pulsed to her core, erupting with a red-hot explosion. Through her sexual overload, she vaguely thought about what a great show she was putting on for all of the spectators tonight. As she floated through her climax, she wondered how many other subs were getting fucked by their masters right now as they enjoyed this spectacle.

Surprisingly, Lukus wasn't chastising her for coming without permission. Instead, the crop continued to rain down on her ass as if he'd missed the entire event, which of course was impossible considering her loud moans. As her first orgasm wrapped up, she could already feel the next building. If he continued like this, she knew it wouldn't be long before he pushed her over the cliff again. She was truthfully not sure how she felt when she heard him throw the riding crop to the stage floor, signaling that at least this phase of the punishment was over. She could have endured a few more strokes if it would've meant coming again.

Her hearing was enhanced from being blindfolded, so she was able to pick up the subtle sounds of Lukus removing his belt as he'd done earlier this afternoon. At the time, he'd belted her to near orgasm only to leave her wriggling with pent up sexual desire. Funny thing was that instead of worrying about how much the belt was going to hurt on her already sore ass, she was readying for the strokes to lead her to her happy place of all-consuming, sub-space orgasms. They were well worth the price of pain required to get there. It flitted through her brain that it was only the promise of these strong orgasms that had tempted her into cheating on Markus with Jake in the first place. She hated how much she needed them.

Lukus's lecture started simultaneously with the first strike of the belt falling hard across her ass. "Why are you being punished, Brianna?"

Through her sobs, she answered with truthful remorse shining through. "Because I did the unthinkable. I cheated on my husband, who I love so very much, and with a total jerk who has hurt me before. I'm so sorry."

"And what the fuck made you do such a stupid and irresponsible thing?"

Another belt stroke rained down on Bri's ass as the inquisition continued. It was distracting to have to answer his questions while fighting to keep the pain and pleasure balance from boiling over inside of her. "I had to. I'd love to blame the blackmail only, but I can't. I love Markus so much, but he was too gentle. Sometimes I *need* to be dominated. Sometimes I *need* the pain, Sir. It takes me to my *happy place*. Thank you, Sir, for letting me go to my *happy place*."

"You'd better thank me, you little pain slut. I think I told you several times today that subs do not have the privilege of coming during a punishment. So, what made you think that coming a few minutes ago was acceptable?"

"I'm so sorry. I couldn't hold it back, Sir. Please, I'm going to come again if you keep belting me like you are. I'm so close. Please, Sir... can I come again?"

"No fucking way. You hold it, do you hear me?"

The next belt connection with her ass was the hardest yet and it pushed her so close to the edge she started to beg. "Please, take a break then. If you keep going, I'll come again. I can't stop it."

"Yes, you can. You need to learn how to control your body. You're a submissive. Like it or not, that means even your orgasms belong to your Dom. I'll tell you when you can and can't get off and right now, you'll hold it and feel the full force of pain you earned by breaking your husband's heart."

Brianna forced her brain to think of something other than the throbbing desire pumping through her pussy right now. She thought about the pain she had caused Markus and how disappointed he must have been in her. She thought about how angry she was at herself for getting sucked into Jake's crappy plan to try to reunite with her. When the hard crack of the belt connecting with the back of her thighs pushed her still closer to tumbling over the edge, she finally resorted to thinking about her grocery list and what household chores she needed to do when she got home.

While those thoughts didn't directly squelch her need to come, the panic over the fact Markus may never let her back in their home to even worry about groceries and cleaning did the trick of dousing her internal fire. With the panic came the full force of the pain and her crying only got worse.

Thank goodness she'd gotten a small measure of control by the time she felt his hands on each of her breasts, gently caressing her until it was time to take off the clamps biting cruelly into her tender nipples. It took several long seconds once the clamps were removed for the blood to reach the tenderized flesh, but when it did, her breasts and nipples felt as if a firecracker had exploded in each punished tip. Coping with the intense pain was threatening to push her into her next free-fall orgasm.

"Oh please, Lukus. I'm begging you. Can you at least take a break... please? It hurts so much when you make me stop from coming."

He silently returned to his job. The next belt strike was even harder to the tender backs of her creamy thighs before she felt him leaning in close. "My name is Master Lukus during a punishment," he growled. "And I haven't reminded you in a while, but you know you have the power to stop this whole thing any time you want. Just safeword and I'll throw down my belt and untie you. Hell, I'll even let you leave with Tiffany, no questions asked."

In her pained haze, it took a few seconds for her to make sense of what he was trying to say. She gasped when she realized he was once again trying to get her to sign the divorce papers. A piece of her heart broke. She had stupidly let her guard down, thinking Lukus had somehow changed his mind about helping Markus get the divorce papers signed. Once Lukus had understood her reasons for cheating, as crazy as they were, he'd gone out to talk to Markus... to try to get through to him about how much she loved him. To have Lukus pushing her to sign the divorce papers again after all they'd been through together today felt like a kick in the gut.

Brianna was having trouble catching her breath, which was only made worse when she could no longer hold back the sobs as fear of Markus's divorcing her came flooding back full force. The renewed fear of her marriage ending was a more powerful punishment than any belting.

She vaguely heard Lukus mutter "Fuck" under his breath and was relieved to hear him throw his belt to the floor, ensuring she'd have at least a few minutes respite before her punishment continued. Still, she was surprised when he began to comfort her in the same way he had during her caning, with a gentle caress of his hand to the small of her back. His touch was like a balm, helping to comfort her.

"Shhh, sweetheart. It's going to be okay."

Damn him. How can he be so hard and punishing one minute and so tender and comforting the next?

His next words were less comforting. "Even if Markus is too stupid to realize what he's losing, you don't need to worry. I'll be happy to keep up your training. We'll have so much fun. I'm a better Dom than Markus ever was anyway."

Brianna's mind raced. What was he trying to say? Did he know Markus wasn't going to forgive her and he was just trying to prepare her? If so, why would he be offering to train her? He was supposed to be getting closer to Tiffany. Was he stupid enough to think she and Tiff would actually get into sharing him? That she was just going to allow him to casually replace her husband who she was still in love with?

She felt his hands caress her ass again. His touch was gentle, but comfort turned into alarm when Lukus went from caressing her ass to nestling into the wet folds of her sex. His first touch was tentative, as if he were unsure if he should proceed, but with each passing moment his touch got bolder until he'd once again plunged several fingers into her cunt while wrapping his other hand around her body to apply pressure to her swollen clit. While the sensations were glorious, Brianna knew it was wrong. She futilely attempted to wrestle free from her bonds, but it was no use.

His hand fell away from the folds of her pussy only to be replaced by him grabbing her by her hip and pressing his hard, fully clothed erection against her ass as he hugged her from behind. His finger stroking her clit didn't miss even a beat as he pulled their bodies as close as possible. The grinding and pumping motion of his hips left little to the imagination as he dry humped her.

She was relieved when she finally found her voice. "My God, what are you doing, Lukus?"

She felt his breath on her cheek as he leaned close. "I'm sorry sweetheart, but you've been teasing me with your naked body all day. I've been ready to explode. I can't hold it in anymore. I need to fuck your sweet pussy."

Her first thought was he was messing with her... teasing her to scare her as part of her punishment. That lasted until he pulled away and she heard him unzipping his pants. He was close enough she could feel his pants as he opened them and pushed them down his body.

It was almost as if she'd left her body and was hovering above the center stage. She had to detach herself from the scene in order to figure out what the hell was going on. Her panic level had skyrocketed.

I trusted him. Lukus swore he'd never hurt me and now he's about to do what Jake would do if he were here... on stage... in front of God only knows how many witnesses who are going to get turned on thinking it's all just part of the show.

A sudden certainty calmed her. The Lukus she had gotten to know today would never, not in a million years, take her against her will. He would die before he would allow anyone, let alone himself, hurt her. Yet, as she felt his rock-hard cock pressed between their bodies, she had to finally admit there was no possible other explanation. He'd clearly just lied to her all day to get her to trust him.

He's just as bad... no... he's worse than Jake. At least Jake never tried to hide what a complete, sadist, selfish jerk he was.

A stray thought flitted through her brain. Thank God she'd found out what a total asshole Lukus was now before he could break Tiffany's heart. It was bad enough Markus and Lukus had both ended up breaking Bri's heart. At least Tiffany would be spared.

That was her final thought before she felt the head of his cock pressing at the opening of her drenched pussy. He'd paused as if he was contemplating if he was really going to proceed. Desperate to get through to him, she called out. "Please, Lukus. What the hell are you doing? Think about it. You can't do this to Markus. You have to stop... *now*."

When he failed to acknowledge her and continued to slide the head of his cock up and down her slick folds, she tried again to reach him. "You're seriously going to rape me? Because that's what this will be if you do this, you know that, right? I can't believe you'd do this to Markus. Fuck that. I can't believe you're going to do this to *me*... to Tiffany. You told me... no... you *promised* me you'd never really hurt me. I trusted you Lukus! I trusted you." Her final words came out in a sobbing plea.

It was as if time stood still for a moment while Bri held her breath, waiting to see if she'd gotten through to him. When she felt the head of his cock pushing against the entrance of her pussy, something inside her snapped. She'd made a promise to herself that she would never again cheat on Markus with another man and right now, that list of men included his best friend taking her against her will. As she felt him sliding inside her, slowly sinking into her wet folds, her heart broke at the loss of not one, but two men she cared deeply for. Both Lukus and Markus had truly deserted her.

In a brief moment of clarity in her otherwise incoherent state, Bri realized she had only one weapon at her disposal. Before she could second-guess the consequences, she pulled the trigger on her weapon. "Divorce! Divorce!" Her scream was piercing. It was so loud, she was sure anyone a block away must have been able to hear her. There could be no mistaking the depth of her conviction at her use of the word. She was relieved the thrusts stopped immediately.

"Markus! Stop! I know you're trying to reclaim her, but you need to stop! It's her safeword!" Lukus's voice was a frantic shout. Even before she interpreted his words, she wondered how he could be talking from so far way when he had his dick buried balls-deep inside of her. Only when she felt the hard cock withdraw from her wet sheath did she truly interpret what Lukus had actually said.

"Markus? Oh my God, Markus, honey... are you here?"

Only silence greeted her, but regardless, she got her answer when she felt way too many hands quickly working to untie both her hands and legs from their tight bondage. Bri's brain was misfiring as she tried to think back to the entire scene on stage.

Is it possible Markus has been here the whole time? Was he the one punishing me tonight?

When she finally found herself free of the bonds holding her up, her legs crumbled under her. Strong arms embraced her, scooping her up and holding her tightly against a muscular chest. Brianna wrapped her arms around him and buried her face into the crook of his neck. That was all it took. Her Markus had come for her. She'd know his yummy Markus scent anywhere.

She was home.

CHAPTER THIRTEEN

MARKUS

Markus sunk to the stage floor, cradling his wife in his arms. He squeezed her tight, afraid to let her go. Twenty-four hours ago, he'd thought he'd never hold her again. He rocked her as she cried against his shoulder. When her tears slowed, he loosened his grip to reach and lift the red blindfold still covering her eyes.

His first glimpse of her beautiful face was an overwhelming relief, despite the tears streaming down her cheeks. He knew the first words he needed to say before anything else.

"I'm so sorry, Bri. I never should have done that to you, sweetheart. I just had to know. If we're going to put this ugly shit behind us, I needed to know you'll never cheat again. I was desperate. This was the only way I could think of to know for sure. I love you so much, it hurts."

He half expected her to be furious at the men's

ruse. He wouldn't blame her if she was. It had been a risky plan. He just prayed she'd give him a chance to explain.

When her tears renewed, he was at a loss. Was she angry at him for leaving her here the night before? Was Lukus wrong about her submission?

Bri finally solved the mystery when she found her words, stammering out her own apology. "I'm sorry, Markus. I'm so *very* sorry. I should have told you that I need to be submissive... at least some of the time. No matter how hard it was for me to talk about. I only pray you can please forgive me."

Gently brushing her tousled hair away from her face, Markus bared his heart. "You aren't the only one to blame. I was a Dom, for Christ's sake. I should have picked up on your cues. I should've been taking better care of you and all your needs. I was just so sure you wanted nothing more to do with pain or the D/s scene after what that asshole did to you. I promise you, things are gonna be different. I just hope you'll give me a chance to fix this."

The love shining back at him from her chocolate-brown eyes calmed him in ways nothing else could as she responded. "Honey, this wasn't your fault. I should have talked to you... told you what I needed. And truly, I don't want everything to change. I love you so much and I love the life we have together. It's just sometimes, not always... well sometimes I just need..." Bri's voice trailed off.

Even now, after all they'd been through in the last twenty-four hours, he could see she still had trouble communicating her desires.

Markus held his fingers to her lips, shushing her. "Bri, we're gonna talk about everything... and not just once, but every single day from now on. We're gonna learn how to communicate with each other so nothing like this ever happens again. But, here... right this minute, all I can think about is getting inside you and finishing what I'd just started. I can't tell you how beautiful you were tonight, sweetheart... tied up... submissive. I never thought it was possible to love you more than I already did, but seeing you tonight, well... "

Brianna didn't let him finish his thought. She lurched forward to press her lips against his, mid-sentence, in a scorching kiss. He groaned with pent up relief as their tongues tangled and his wife ground her naked body against him in an attempt to hump him. Their kiss was so hot, it felt like it had the power to literally weld them back together.

The urge to be inside her wouldn't be denied. He need to re-stake his claim on her—to replace any lingering memory she might have of the asshole Davenport's brief possession. Taking charge, Markus rolled Brianna to her back, pressing her naked body into the stage floor. Her yelp as her punished ass cheeks made contact with the hard wood floor was like music to his sadist ears. The feral desire shining back at him from her expressive eyes only fed his need more.

Throwing all caution and tenderness aside, Markus grabbed Bri's ankles, yanking them up and over her head, opening up her core to his mercy. Without prompting, Bri wrapped her arms around her legs so her ankles were resting over her head, near her ears. It was the most gorgeous sight he'd ever seen. His wife, the love of his life, and now his submissive—her slick pussy open and available for the taking.

He already felt like he was ready to explode, and he hadn't sunk into her yet. He slid the head of his erection through her wet folds, ensuring she was ready for him. He warned her, growling, "Hold tight, sweetheart. Later, I'm going to make sweet love to you over and over, but right now, I can't wait another minute. I'm gonna remind this body of yours who it belongs to."

As their eyes devoured each other, Markus lunged forward, plunging his rock-hard cock balls-deep in his wife. Their joint scream of ecstasy was intoxicating and only spurred on their desperate need for each other. Markus set a fast pace as he pulled out of his wife again and again, only to surge forward harder and faster with each thrust. Their eyes never left each other as their bodies reclaimed their mate. He pushed down his vulnerability as emotional tears streamed down his cheeks, comforted by the tears in his wife's eyes as they reconnected in the most intimate of ways.

The sex was just too hot to last for long. It only took a few minutes of fast fucking before they were both on the verge of coming.

"Yes, that's it, Markus. You feel perfect. I needed this so bad." Bri's breathing was ragged.

Possessive insecurities flared. "You're mine... *only* mine. Do you hear me, Brianna?" His tone of voice left no room for negotiation.

"Yes... oh God yes. Only yours, Markus."

"You feel so tight. So fucking perfect. Come with me, sweetheart. Let it go now. I've got you."

Markus had never, in all his life, had an orgasm like he had at that moment. The combination of love for his wife and relief of not losing her combined with his pent-up desire to send him flying. Bri's face blurred behind the white stars that exploded just as he spurted his load of hot cum deep in her womb. His guttural grunt was that of a man in ecstasy. The only thing that could make the moment better was watching the woman he loved falling into her own powerful climax.

Suddenly exhausted, he slumped into Brianna, dragging a groan from the woman literally folded in half under him. Markus finally rolled off his wife to lie on his back on the floor next to her, letting her bring her legs down before pulling her tight against his body. Neither of them wanted to stop touching each other and they spent a few minutes just catching their breath.

Only after they'd reluctantly returned to earth did Brianna bury her face against his chest and whisper, "I can't believe we just did that in front of an audience."

He chuckled, hugging her closer before whispering playfully back. "Don't worry. It was a rather paltry crowd tonight and I somehow don't think they'll mind the show considering they're our best friends."

She clearly didn't understand what he meant because Bri lifted herself off his chest to bravely glance out to see how big the crowd was. Markus followed her gaze as they both saw a tied-up Tiffany as the only patron. Even from this distance, Markus could see Tiff looked as big of a mess as Bri was. Her eyes were red and puffy from crying and she had it worse because of the large ball-gag forcing her silence. He watched as his wife and her best friend stared back and forth, each trying to communicate from afar.

Bri finally glanced back at him, a look of awe and confusion on her beautiful face. Markus answered her unasked question. "I didn't want an audience for this. Lukus was nice enough to close down the club at the last minute for us."

Her eyes widened with surprise. He could tell she'd been so busy reuniting with him, she'd forgotten the role his own best friend had played in the night's events. Bri glanced around the stage, first stopping to watch Derek and Rachel, still fucking like rabbits near the back of the stage. Markus had to admire his friend's strength at lifting his wife up off his erection as he held her in his arms before letting gravity slam her back down, impaling her over and over.

Forcing her attention away from the real-life porno, Bri continued to look around until she found Lukus. He was sitting at the end of the gynecological table, watching the events on stage play out with interest. Markus fought down a pang of jealousy as he watched his wife break into one of her gorgeous smiles as her eyes met his best friend's across the stage.

Lukus didn't return the smile, and Markus, knowing him so well, knew exactly why. Their plan had skirted Lukus's comfort zone. Remembering the shock on Lukus's face as Brianna had called out her safeword, Markus realized just how much he'd asked of his friend that night. He and Bri owed Lukus their marriage, and Markus vowed in that moment to make sure he found some way to repay his old roommate.

Bri tore her eyes away long enough to look back at her husband. "Markus, I need to go talk to Lukus for a minute, and then can we please go home?"

The thought of having to drive all the way back home didn't sound like the best plan. "I don't know. I'm not sure we'll be able to make it all the way home before we need to *make up* again. I was kind of hoping you'd agree to stay over in one of Lukus's guest rooms tonight."

A grin lit up his wife's face. "That sounds wonderful, as long as you don't make me sleep in the damn slave cage again."

Her words gut-punched him. The grateful feelings of minutes ago evaporated at the thought of Brianna the night before. "He made you sleep in a fucking cage?" he ground out, sending a death glare in Lukus's direction.

Bri placed her hand over his chest, trying to placate him. "Honey, what did you expect? You had to know what kind of a place you were leaving me in, right?" Markus wasn't sure if he was angrier at himself or Lukus in that moment. Bri kept trying to calm him down. "It's okay, Markus. It was what I needed at the time. As terrible as the last twenty-four hours have been, they needed to happen to get us to where we are right now. Please, don't be mad at Lukus. He was really great to me, all things considered."

Markus took several deep breaths, trying to come to terms with how utterly he had failed his wife the night before. No words would fix things, but he had to try. "You're right. God help me, but I was so angry and hurt last night I didn't care what was going to happen to you." Cupping her cheek softly, he added, "I'm so sorry I put you through this and I know you're right. We both owe Lukus a lot, even if he did put you in a fucking cage. But you only get a minute now. You can talk to him more tomorrow."

Bri leaned in to give her husband a tender kiss before pushing off him to stand on wobbly legs. Markus stood as well, watching has his wife walked over to where Lukus was sitting, looking as if he were awaiting his doom. Even while she was still many feet away Lukus started his apology. "I'm so sorry, Brianna. That didn't really play out exactly as I thought it would. I won't blame you if you never trust me again."

Brianna just kept walking straight into his arms. Markus again pushed down his own insecurities of seeing his naked wife in the arms of another man. At least this time, it was a man that was like a brother to him. He approached them just as Brianna responded. "Lukus, don't you dare feel guilty about anything. Yes, tonight was pretty shitty, but don't forget, I set this into motion. I was the one who went with Jake, and I was the one who deserved to be punished. If this is what it took to get Markus to believe I won't ever cheat again, then so be it. I'm just so relieved that I hadn't been wrong about you earlier. I couldn't believe it when... well... when I thought you would actually..."

"Rape you?" Lukus asked incredulously. "I can't believe you considered it for even one second.

Seriously, it was so obvious it was Markus." His friend defended.

"No, it wasn't. It wasn't obvious at all." Brianna argued back.

Finally, Lukus broke into a broad grin. "Must you argue with me in every single conversation? Surely you know I would cut off my right arm before I'd ever let anyone else, let alone myself, hurt you like that, sweetheart. If you've learned nothing else, please know that. All you have to do is call and I'll be there for you. Markus is one lucky bastard. I can't wait to watch him trying to tame you." He didn't even try to hide his smirk as the men's gaze met over Brianna's head.

"I feel like I should invest in a good donut pillow to sit on. I think my ass is gonna need it." The sound of his wife's chuckle broke the tension.

Lukus's hearty laugh helped Markus start to finally feel like things were truly going to be okay. When Bri hugged him again, Lukus teased her. "You get going now and have fun making up with my best friend. I'd use the guest room at the far end of the hall if I were you. One, because I want you as far away from my room as possible so I don't hear you two fucking each other senseless all night, but more importantly because Derek and Rachel used the other guest room earlier and I have no idea what kind of a mess you might find in there."

"Thanks, Lukus... really... for everything."

Markus was standing right behind Bri when

Lukus replied. "You're welcome, sweetheart. I'll see you tomorrow. Now get going before Markus blows a gasket." He looked over Bri's shoulder again to smile at his best friend.

Markus defended himself. "I'm not gonna blow a gasket. I'm with Brianna. We owe you a lot, my friend. Thanks for coming out to the house today to knock some sense into me." Markus reached out to shake his old roommate's hand, but Lukus jumped down from the table and pulled Markus into a man-hug instead.

"I told you. You're like a brother to me, man," clapping Markus on the back.

When the man-hug turned awkward, the men stepped apart and without warning, Markus stooped low to throw Bri over his shoulder. When she giggled and tried to wiggle free, he used his free hand to slap her punished ass.

"Oweee, Markus. My butt really hurts," she complained.

"I'm sure it does. I think you'd better get used to that, sweetheart. I see a few punishments in your future."

The fact that his wife giggled happily at the thought of being disciplined by him was a gift he'd never expected. It was going to take him some time to get his Dom legs back under him, but excitement sparked as he realized how much fun they were going to have exploring D/s together.

CHAPTER FOURTEEN

L ukus watched his best friend leaving with trepidation. As thrilled as he was at how things had turned out for Markus and Brianna, he knew they'd come close to having a real disaster on their hands tonight—a disaster that could have caused Brianna to lose her trust in both men. In retrospect, the plan had been too risky. Even now, knowing Brianna forgave him, he was holding his breath, afraid to turn around and face Tiffany. His little stunt tonight just might have been too much for her to take.

I should've called a fucking cab and forced her to go home. What the fuck was I thinking having her watch tonight? This was hard core and Tiffany's a newbie.

Once Bri and Markus were gone, he knew he couldn't stall any longer. It was time to pay the piper. Taking a deep breath to steel himself for what was to come, he turned around, finally let his gaze fall on Tiffany. The sight of her took his breath away. He felt a few seconds of light-headedness as he took in the visage of the beautiful woman staring back at him.

He stood grounded to his spot, unable to move or tear his gaze away from hers, as he tried to analyze exactly why she was affecting him so. After all, she was fully clothed, not naked as so many subs regularly were at the club. Her eyes were red and puffy, and her nose was running. Drool spilled from around the too-large ball-gag. It'd clearly been overflowing for some time because in the dim lighting of the theater, he could make out the wetness on the front of her low-cut dress. She painted a wonderfully submissive image that stirred every protective bone in his body.

Damn, I want her so bad it hurts.

What finally drew his attention away from her body was the intensity of her glare. Never wavering. Never backing down. It made him wonder if she planned to deck him the minute he let her loose.

I guess that's okay. I deserve it this time. Fuck, I hope she doesn't just walk out.

As he approached Tiffany, her gaze reminded him of just how precarious things were between them. He dropped to eye level and began to untie her, saving the ball-gag for last since he suspected he was going to get an earful once she could talk. He dreaded what she had to say.

Just before he removed the gag, he reflected on how odd it was to feel so uncertain... even vulnerable. He recognized that for once in his life, he was not the one in control... not in the slightest. This little spitfire sitting in front of him might not have realized it yet, but she figuratively had him by the balls. She could walk out the door hating his guts and he'd have no choice but to accept it.

Their eyes were locked as he reached around her to unbuckle the strap holding the gag in her mouth. Once free, Tiffany spent a minute flexing her jaw slowly in an attempt to get the kinks out. Lukus pulled the red silk scarf out of his back pocket and was relieved when she didn't smack his hand away as he reached out to wipe the remnants of tears and smeared mascara from her face. She even allowed him to hold the scarf to her nose.

"Blow for me."

She hesitated, but finally blew her nose quite loudly, making him smile. "Good girl."

It was silly, but he was pleased she let him perform such an intimate service for her. When fresh, fat tears began to fall from her bright eyes, Lukus reached out with the pad of his thumb to wipe them away. At the feel of his touch, anger flashed in her watery eyes. In a flash, Lukus found himself knocked backwards onto his ass. He luckily got his hands behind him in time to prevent being laid out flat on his back.

Having launched herself like a projectile out of her chair, Tiffany knocked Lukus to the ground and like a woman crazed, began pelting his chest with her fists as she allowed her pent-up anger to come out in the form of a flailing rant.

"You, asshole! I can't even believe you did that to me—to Brianna! You tied me up... left me here... alone... to watch my best friend be punished— tortured by you and her husband. Just because things turned out okay doesn't excuse what you did. She thought you were raping her... just like Jake used to. What kind of man does something like that? I'll tell you... an asshole... a barbarian... a complete... fucking... jerk. A... a... well, I'm so upset I can't think of any more names, but as soon as I do, I'll let you have it again you big... big... *dummy*."

He tried hard not to smile—he really did—but she was just too damn cute. His grin only enraged her more until Lukus was forced to lock her tightly to his chest, holding her flailing arms immobile until she finally started to settle down. Her breath was coming hard and heavy from her exertion and he held her tight, waiting for her to calm down.

After a few minutes, he loosened his hold. "Are you feeling better now?"

"No." She was pouting, and it was adorable.

Time to do some serious groveling, sport.

"Okay. For what it's worth, I'm sorry Tiffany. You're completely right. Tonight's plan was too risky. It really could have backfired and ended up hurting Brianna. I've already apologized to her and now I'm apologizing to you. I made a mistake. I should have packed your beautiful ass in a cab and forced you to leave when I had the chance. But I didn't... and I can only hope you'll forgive me. I do want to point out, in my own defense, we did get the outcome everyone wanted. I helped Markus and Brianna... um... *make up.* Now it's up to them to learn how to actually talk to each other." He waited expectantly, holding his breath for her answer.

Tiffany got a strange, far-away look on her face before she replied. "It really was amazing watching them... well, you know... *make up.*"

Lukus felt the shift of the ground beneath him as the power began to change hands. He was more aware than ever of her sitting in his lap. Her proximity was intoxicating. "Yeah, it was one of the hottest scenes I've ever witnessed and that's saying something for me considering I own the club."

It was pretty dark on the floor, but he could detect her blush as she remembered how hot it had been to watch Markus and Brianna's unbridled passion as they had their make-up fuck. It took all of his will power to keep from trying to duplicate the scene with Tiffany here on the floor of the audience pit. It was quick, but he was sure the idea had just been flitting across Tiffany's mind as well. Despite just meeting her, he could read her expressive face so easily.

Still, he wasn't interested in a quick fuck. Not with Tiffany. That realization forced him to take the high road. "So, now that the show is over, you want to come back upstairs? I never gave you the tour of the loft. It's been almost a year since I've had a Saturday night off from the club. Maybe we could chill out... watch a movie or something." He worked to keep his voice steady, trying hard not to let her see just how much he wanted her to come back upstairs with him.

Indecision flitted across her revealing face. "I don't know, Lukus. I'm not sure that's a good idea. Let's face it; we come from pretty different backgrounds and... well... I'm not sure how I feel about all of this." She waved her hand through the air to indicate the club.

"The Pit is just one part of my life, Tiffany. It doesn't define me."

"But you're a Dom."

"Yes, I am. But I'm still a man, and you're a very beautiful woman. Not to mention, I'm pretty sure there's at least a little bit of submissive in you trying to get out. I'd love to be the one to coax her out and show her what she's been missing."

Anxiety crept into her gaze. The fear in her eyes was strangely unsettling for the Dom. Lukus wanted to reassure her, but he didn't know how. Taking a chance, he leaned in the few inches separating them. He wanted to kiss her, taste her, comfort her.

She stopped him with a firm hand on his chest as he got close. "Stop. I can't do this." Tiffany pushed away from him and struggled to her feet. She was acting erratic, distracted. She'd somehow lost one of her high-heeled sandals in the fray and stooped to grab it and put it on.

Lukus detected her rising panic and knew she was gonna bolt. He fought the urge to demand she stay. He had to remind himself he didn't have the right to stop her, at least not yet. Maybe never. He pushed off the floor to stand just in time to catch Tiffany as she lost her balance hopping to put on her errant shoe.

"Damn, my legs still feel like Jell-O."

He didn't even try to hide the desire he felt for her anymore, pulling her close enough to feel his rock-hard cock pressed against her. If she was gonna leave, he wanted her to know it was her choice, not his.

They stayed close in their tight embrace, locked together in body and through their penetrating stare. He could see the internal battle in her eyes. She was feeling lost. He wanted so much to help her, but he felt like he'd just be acting like a self-serving asshole. Still, he had to try. "I really want you to stay, Tiff. Not because I want to fuck you...

well no, that's not true. I *definitely* want to fuck you. Wait... that came out wrong. *Fuck...*"

It was Tiffany's turn to smile at him and his insecure rant. "It's nice to know I'm not the only one feeling off base here."

"Off base? Hell, I'm in completely uncharted territory here woman, and you aren't helping matters at all playing hard to get."

"I'm not playing, Lukus. You have me so confused. We barely know each other, yet I've never wanted anyone as much as I want you right this minute. But then what? What happens tomorrow? The next day? What happens when things blow up in our faces and then we have to see each other when Markus and Bri invite us both over for a barbecue? I'm not into one-night stands, and I'm certainly not into sharing with other... what would you call them? Women? Subs? Slaves?"

"We haven't even given this a shot yet. And even if things would work out, I'm not asking you to share me, Tiff. I'm not with anyone right now and I told you earlier; I've been in monogamous relationships before."

"Really? For how long? A year?" Tiffany studied his face closely and when he remained silent, she continued on with her guessing. "Six months? Oh my God." Looking panicked she finally guessed, "Three months? Am I even close?" When Lukus stayed silent, she flung her arms in the air, trying to push away from him. "Never mind, don't answer that. I have my answer. You'll never be able to do what Markus did for Brianna."

Lukus reached to grab her close again. "Well considering Markus fucked everything up with Brianna, I sure as hell hope not."

"I'm not talking about that. I'm talking about settling for just me when you can have any woman —hell, as many women—as you want here at the club. Women who will gladly do anything and everything you want from them without being afraid."

"Tiffany Lauren O'Sullivan." When she looked surprised at his use of her whole name he continued. "Yes, baby. I took the time to ask Brianna for your full name before the show started." He loved that she looked pleased. "What makes you think the words *settle* and *you* belong in the same sentence? Call it a sixth sense, but I somehow just know I would never be settling to be with you. Did you ever think I'm the one with a boatload of baggage and maybe you'd be settling to be with me?"

Her breath was ragged. Lukus suspected their proximity was starting to get to her. He wasn't surprised when she finally whispered, "Lukus... I'm scared."

He brushed her cheek lightly with the backs of his fingers before gently pushing a stray wisp of hair behind her ear. "You can't be even half as scared as I am, Tiffany. I don't know what's happened to me since I met you, but I swear, you've knocked me on my ass. You have me acting like a fucking teenager instead of a Dom because I don't want to scare you away. Please, can't you at least give us half a chance before you throw it away?"

Several long seconds ticked by as they sized each other up before Tiffany finally seemed to come to some kind of conclusion. Her smile got bigger by the second. "So, you have a movie theater. It's been a while since I went to a movie. I think I'd better check it out."

His relief was palpable. "I even have a theater-style popcorn machine. If you're a good girl, I'll make you some popcorn."

Her smile was contagious. "I'm always a good girl."

Lukus was laughing. "Oh, I beg to differ. I've seen you and Bri in action. You're both sassy little balls of fire."

"Thank you... I think?"

Lukus took her hand and they slowly made their way up the stairs to the stage, on their way to his loft. They were just about to where Markus and Brianna had begun to *make up* when Tiffany stopped walking, dragging him to a stop. She didn't say a word, but she didn't have to. Lukus could see the passion in her eyes. He saw her temptation. Did she want him to take her there just as Markus had taken Brianna?

Her uncertainty flickered once again on her

expressive face, warring inside her. Lukus pulled her into his arms, holding her gaze... holding off kissing her as long as he could. He felt an urge to make this moment last. Finally, when he could hold back no more, he lowered his lips to hers in what began as a tender kiss. He reveled in how perfectly their bodies molded together as he pulled her curves tightly against him, making her his willing captive. While one hand held her waist against him, he couldn't resist the urge to let his other hand drift lower to boldly cup that beautiful ass he'd been admiring since the moment he'd set eyes on her.

It didn't take long for the gentle kiss to turn into all-out passion as Lukus slipped his tongue into the depths of her mouth, exploring and enjoying her purrs of pleasure. His heart thumped so hard, it felt like it could pound out of his chest. No woman had ever made him feel like this with a simple kiss... *ever*. It was his turn to be afraid. He wanted her bad, but he didn't want to fuck this up. When he felt her grinding against him, he knew the time had come. He needed to do one final thing before he let this go any further. Earlier he'd planned to do it more as a small joke, but now... how he felt this very minute... it was no longer a joke. It was important.

Tiffany's eyes widened when Lukus pulled out of their passionate kiss. He was pleased to see how much their kiss had been affecting her. Her chest was rising and falling as she gasped to catch her breath.

I hope you know what the hell you're doing, sport. This could really blow up in your face.

"So, before we take this any farther, isn't there something you forgot to tell me?" He tried to keep his tone light, although he was as nervous as hell.

"Like what, exactly?" Her voice was still breathy.

"I love how you gave *me* the third degree about being in a monogamous relationship, but isn't there something you're forgetting to tell me about your own relationships, Miss O'Sullivan?"

He was actually thrilled when she continued to look lost. It told him he hadn't been reading her wrong. He knew the second she realized what he was getting at. The panic in her eyes was palpable. He just wished he knew exactly what she was afraid of.

"Oh, my God. Wait. I was going to break up with him as soon as I talked to him tomorrow. I had already made up my mind."

He hated how relieved he felt. "Sure, you say that now, but I think you were just about to cheat on Jonathan or Jack or whatever the hell his name is. I don't appreciate being the other man. Not to mention, I don't think this is a very good way to start things off with us... with a lie." He paused for dramatic effect before flashing his most devilish smile. "You've been a very naughty girl,

Tiffany. I think you've just earned your first punishment."

Her answer came out in a panicked whoosh. "*Oh, crap.*"

It was a good thing he still held her tightly because at his words, her knees buckled from under her. "Whoa, there. I've got you, baby."

It felt like they were both holding their breath... sizing each other up... figuring out exactly how the next few minutes were going to play out. The power dynamics at play between them felt important, like they were laying the foundation for the future.

Tiffany's breath was labored. The look on her face fluctuated between fear, excitement, and guilt. Lukus finally decided it was time to put her out of her misery. Reaching into the pocket of his jeans, he fished out Tiffany's cell phone he'd asked Derek to retrieve from her car after dinner. He held it up, expectantly, in front of her. "You have a decision to make. I'm not interested in a one-night stand with you either, Tiffany, and I'm certainly not interested in sharing you with Joe or Jeff or whatever the fuck his name is. You want this to happen, then you have a call to make."

Her eyes were wide. "Right now? Isn't it enough that I'll call him tomorrow?"

"Not if you want to stay here. I want this settled. Do you still have feelings for him?"

"No. Honestly, I never really did."

"Well then, this shouldn't be too hard of a decision then, should it?"

"But... you said... I mean... what are you going to do?" Her voice trailed off.

The Dom had returned to the building when he spoke authoritatively. "Take the phone, Tiffany. Call him... right now so we can get on with our night."

Her face registered her surprise at the tone of his request. It was brief, but he caught it... her hint of a smile before she quietly acquiesced with a simple, "Yes, Sir." As soon as the words left her mouth, she smiled broadly, and it was all Lukus could do to keep from throwing her to the floor right that minute. Two simple little words, and yet they spoke volumes to the Dom.

When she tentatively reached out for her phone, their eyes were locked. She glanced down at the phone to find Jason's number in her contact list. She hit send and then returned to stare up into Lukus's green eyes. Several long seconds went by when Lukus thought her call was going to go to voicemail until she finally started talking. What he would give to hear both sides of the conversation.

"Jason... hey... yeah it's me. I know. I'm sorry I didn't call you earlier, but something really big came up and well... I really hate to do this over the phone like this, but I need to tell you I don't want to see you anymore." At least thirty-seconds float by, their eyes never leaving each other's while Tiffany listened to Jason, presumably trying to talk her out of breaking up. "Like I said, I'm sorry if I'm hurting you, but really, I don't want to go out anymore. No, it's not really you. It's just... well..." As she paused, Lukus flashed her his biggest smile for moral support. "No Jason, honestly... I've met someone... someone I really want to get to know a lot better and I don't want to start a new relationship with this hanging between us. I'm sorry, but I need to go now. Good luck." Tiffany didn't give Jason half a chance to change her mind. She simply hit END.

"Good girl. How do you feel?"

"Honestly... relieved. Even without meeting you, it was never going to work with Jason."

"I'm glad to hear that. Now, I think we need to get going upstairs."

Tiffany stayed planted in her spot, causing Lukus to turn back to look at her. "But... what about..."

He quickly held his fingers up to shush her. "Don't worry about anything. We have plenty of time. I know what you're thinking and don't worry your beautiful little ass about the punishment, at least not right now. Let's just say we're going to park that for a while and come back to it later... tomorrow... maybe next week. We're just gonna take things slow and we'll both know when it's time to talk about it again, okay?"

Tiffany visibly relaxed and Lukus took her hand, trying to move them towards his loft, but she stayed grounded to the spot. When he turned back to face her, he could see the passion had returned to her beautiful blue eyes. He hated to disappoint her, but he just couldn't do it. Not here.

"Baby, I really want us to go upstairs now."

"But Lukus, I thought we could just stay here for a bit longer."

God, he hated this, but she deserved to hear the truth. "I know what you want Tiffany, and honestly, I'm tempted, but... well..." Should he continue even though it would hurt her? He had to be honest. "Baby, this is gonna sound shocking and I truly wish there was a better way to say it, but I don't know what that might be, so I'm just going to tell you the truth and hope you understand. I want you so bad right now, but I don't want our first time to be here... on this stage. I..." Their eyes were locked together.

God, I hate to say these next words. I pray she doesn't just tell me to fuck off.

"I've punished and fucked too many other women here on the stage. You're special, Tiff. I want us to go upstairs... to snuggle... to watch a movie and eat popcorn... to maybe make love... maybe not. The point is, you deserve better than a fast fuck on the dirty floor of the stage. Don't you see? Going upstairs to the loft... just the two of us... that's special. That's where we belong tonight."

The shocked look on her face only lasted a few seconds before she let loose a high pitch squeal just before launching herself into his arms, almost knocking him over.

"Oh, Lukus. That's the most romantic thing anyone has ever said to me."

It was a good thing he had a strong hold on her, because she lifted up her legs and wrapped them around his waist, trapping their bodies together. Lukus chuckled as she started pelting his face and neck with quick, sweet kisses. He turned to head to the elevator with her wrapped in his arms when he felt her start sucking on his neck.

I guess you said the right thing after all, sport. Now... let's see if she'll stay more than an hour before bolting from the building.

The End

To Be Continued in Book Three, Having it All
Release Date 9/22/20 - Available Now in Pre-order

BLURB for *Having it All* - Book Three

Submission is an addiction she thought she'd left behind, but who can say no to him?

Best friends are always supposed to be there for

each other, but walking into a place like The Punishment Pit was above and beyond.

Now Master Lukus is holding her captive, intent on punishing Tiffany for her mistakes, and instead of saving Brianna, she's trapped with a man from her darkest fantasies.

Tiffany's in way over her head. Falling too hard, too fast.
And the dangerously dominant owner of the club is pushing all her buttons, waking up every naughty desire she'd ever had and more.

Here's a little taste of Having it All:

Lukus

Lukus was just about to crawl out of his skin after waiting for what seemed like an eternity for Tiffany to join him in the theater. He'd distracted himself by making popcorn and going through his movie collection to find the films he and Tiffany talked about earlier. He figured he'd let her choose her favorite, since he planned on spending the whole night watching her instead of the movie anyway. He'd already dimmed the lights for a romantic setting.

He was behind the bar mixing a Jack and Coke when he caught movement out of the corner of his eye. He glanced up as he poured the Coke to welcome Tiff to the theater and froze.

"Fuck me." A low growl accompanied his expletive. He stood frozen in place as he caught his first glimpse of Tiffany just inside the door to the room. She was definitely *not* in the Harley T-shirt he'd left out on the bed. In fact, courtesy of the side lamp she was standing directly in front of, he could see she was definitely *not* wearing his boxer shorts either. The back lighting was perfectly outlining her very curvy, very naked, body through his now favorite dress shirt.

She's so fucking hot. I'm gonna remember this moment every time I wear that shirt.

"Ah, damn it." Lukus had no choice but to tear his attention away from Tiff as the Coke he was pouring overflowed the glass, making a mess on the bar. He could hear Tiffany giggling as he reached to grab a bar towel to try to sop up the drink before it dripped onto the carpet. Only when he had the spill contained did he glance back up to see Tiffany walking slowly towards him, a totally naughty smile on her face. She took a seat on the high barstool across from him.

"What's the problem, Lukus? Looks like you're making a mess back there. Are you sure you know what you're doing?" Her voice was soft and playful.

"I'm not sure about me, but I can see by that

twinkle in your eye, young lady, that you *absolutely* know what you're doing, you little minx."

Her eyes darted around nervously before Tiffany quietly answered, "Don't be so sure. Looks can be deceiving. Truthfully, I feel so nervous that I've nearly forgotten why I'm still here."

Her vulnerability cut through his chest like a knife. Leaning forward to place his forearms on the bar, Lukus moved in closer to stare into her ocean-blue eyes before answering her in a voice that left no room for doubt. "Well then. Let me remind you. You're here because this is exactly where you belong tonight. I know it. You know it. I just wish you'd stop fighting it, baby."

"Easy for you to say. This is your house. This is just another day for you." She took a short break. He could see she was debating if she really wanted to continue on with her thought. He patiently waited her out until she finally continued. "I don't think you have a clue just how close I came to putting my dress back on and sneaking out to my car."

Even in the dim lighting, it was easy for Lukus to see her uncertainty was back. He stood and walked around the end of the bar until he was directly behind her barstool. Tiff made no attempt to turn herself around to face him, so Lukus took the opportunity to reach out and smooth down a few escaped wisps of her silky hair. He finally swiveled her barstool around so that she was facing him.

He leaned forward, placing his hands on either side of her on the backrest, effectively trapping her. Lukus leaned his body forward against her, happy when she subconsciously opened her legs to draw him in as he pressed close. When their faces were just a few inches apart, Tiffany quickly closed her eyes, apparently deciding his stare was too intense.

"Open your eyes, Tiffany." When she didn't comply, Lukus reached up to cup her cheek with his hand, stroking her gently with his thumb. When he detected her leaning slightly into his hand, seeking out his intimacy, he repeated his request. "Open your eyes, baby... please." His voice was soft, careful not to spook her.

When Tiffany finally opened her eyes, he could see the glossy sheen of her tears. He continued to speak gently. "First, thank you for being honest with me about wanting to leave. This will never work if you hide your feelings from me. Now, if you feel uncomfortable at my place, that's okay. I can fix that. I can take you home to your place or to a neutral downtown hotel with lots of wonderful amenities to spoil you. Just tell me where you'll feel comfortable and I'll make it happen. But walking away is not an option, Tiffany. I won't allow that to happen. I'm not letting you out of my sight until we can get a handle on whatever the hell it is that's happening between us."

When she remained silent, he continued. "And for the record, you couldn't be more wrong. The fact you think this is just a normal day for me just proves you don't know me as well as you seem to think you do. Maybe—just maybe—you should give me the benefit of the doubt until I prove I don't deserve it. You think you can do that?"

He could see the hope flicker in her eyes. He detected her slight nod as her only reply.

"So, where's all that sass now, Miss O'Sullivan?" he asked, grinning. "You've got me hooked on your beautiful, sassy mouth. Don't tell me you're all out of jibes for me."

He knew he'd succeeded at breaking through her defenses when Tiff's shy smile returned.

"Oh, don't worry. I'll never run out of sass. Maybe I'm just being careful to use it more wisely. After all, I'm not entirely sure I understand all the rules of the game we're playing."

Lukus was suddenly serious again. "Oh baby, that's your whole problem. This isn't a game, at least not for me. Nothing has felt this real to me in a very long time."

Tiff sucked in a sharp breath, surprised by his admission. "Why me, Lukus? Seriously..."

Lukus moved his fingers to her lips, effectively shushing her. "Stop. Enough analyzing. We have plenty of time for that later. Tonight, let it be enough to know it's because you look amazing in my favorite shirt."

Tiff's mischievous smile told him she was pleased. "This is really your favorite shirt?"

Lukus's smile turned predatory. "It is now."

To Be Continued in Book Three, Having it All
Release Date 9/22/20 - Available Now in Pre-order

USA Today Bestselling Author Livia Grant lives in Chicago with her husband and furry rescue dog named Max. She is fortunate to have been able to travel extensively and as much as she loves to visit places around the globe, the Midwest and its changing seasons will always be home. Livia's readers appreciate her riveting stories filled with deep, character driven plots, often spiced with elements of BDSM.

- Livia's Website: http://www.liviagrant.com/
- Join Livia's Facebook Group: The Passion Vault
- Facebook Author Page to Like: https://www.facebook.com/pages/Livia-Grant/877459968945358
- Goodreads: https://www.goodreads.com/author/show/8474605.Livia_Grant
- BookBub: https://www.bookbub.com/profile/livia-grant

Connect to Livia's books through her website here.

Black Light Series

Infamous Love, A Black Light Prequel

Black Light: Rocked

Black Light: Valentine Roulette

Black Light: Rescued

Black Light: Roulette Redux

Complicated Love

Black Light: Celebrity Roulette

Black Light: Purged

Black Light: Scandalized

Black Light: Roulette War

Black Light: The Beginning

Black Light: Rolled - coming September, 2020

Punishment Pit Series

Wanting it All - Now Available

Securing it All - Release 9/1/20

Having it All - Release 9/22/20

Balancing it All - Release 10/6/20

Defending it All - Release 10/27/20

Protecting it All - Release 11/17/20

Expecting it All - Release 12/1/20

Stand Alone Books

Blessed Betrayal

Royalty, American Style

Alpha's Capture (as Livia Bourne)

Blinding Salvation (as Livia Bourne)

Don't miss Livia's next book!

Sign-up for Livia's Newsletter

Follow Livia on BookBub

BLACK COLLAR PRESS

Black Collar Press is a small publishing house started by authors Livia Grant and Jennifer Bene in late 2016. The purpose was simple - to create a place where the erotic, kinky, and exciting worlds they love to explore could thrive and be joined by other like-minded authors.

If this is something that interests you, please go to the Black Collar Press website and read through the FAQs. If your questions are not answered there, please contact us directly at: blackcollarpress@gmail.com

Where to find Black Collar Press:

- Website: http://www. blackcollarpress.com/
- Facebook: https://www. facebook.com/blackcollarpress/

- Twitter: https:// twitter.com/BlackCollarPres
- Black Light East and West may be fictitious, but you can now join our very real Facebook Group for Black Light Fans - Black Light Central

Made in the USA
Columbia, SC
08 February 2021